## THE Essential COLLECTION

*New York Times* and *USA TODAY* Bestselling Author

# DIANA PALMER

D0508037

**Harlequin**®

TORONTO NEW YORK LONDON
AMSTERDAM PARIS SYDNEY HAMBURG
STOCKHOLM ATHENS TOKYO MILAN MADRID
PRAGUE WARSAW BUDAPEST AUCKLAND

To my very special friend Suzanne Hewstone

Recycling programs
for this product may
not exist in your area.

ISBN-13: 978-0-373-36369-8

EVAN

Copyright © 1991 by Diana Palmer

All rights reserved. Except for use in any review, the reproduction or
utilization of this work in whole or in part in any form by any electronic,
mechanical or other means, now known or hereafter invented, including
xerography, photocopying and recording, or in any information storage
or retrieval system, is forbidden without the written permission of the
publisher, Harlequin Enterprises Limited, 225 Duncan Mill Road,
Don Mills, Ontario, Canada, M3B 3K9.

This is a work of fiction. Names, characters, places and incidents are
either the product of the author's imagination or are used fictitiously,
and any resemblance to actual persons, living or dead, business
establishments, events or locales is entirely coincidental.

This edition published by arrangement with Harlequin Books S.A.

For questions and comments about the quality of this book
please contact us at Customer_eCare@Harlequin.ca.

® and TM are trademarks of the publisher. Trademarks indicated with
® are registered in the United States Patent and Trademark Office, the
Canadian Trade Marks Office and in other countries.

www.eHarlequin.com

**Printed in U.S.A.**

AVAILABLE JUNE 2011

*A Long, Tall Texan Summer*
(containing "Tom," "Drew" and "Jobe")
*Nora*
*Dream's End*
*Champagne Girl*
*Friends and Lovers*
*The Wedding in White*

AVAILABLE JULY 2011

*Heather's Song*
*Snow Kisses*
*To Love and Cherish*
*Long, Tall and Tempted*
(containing "Redbird," "Paper Husband" and
"Christmas Cowboy")
*The Australian*
*Darling Enemy*
*Trilby*

AVAILABLE AUGUST 2011

*Sweet Enemy*
*Soldier of Fortune*
*The Tender Stranger*
*Enamored*
*After the Music*
*The Patient Nurse*

AVAILABLE SEPTEMBER 2011

*The Case of the Mesmerizing Boss*
*The Case of the Confirmed Bachelor*
*The Case of the Missing Secretary*
*September Morning*
*Diamond Girl*
*Eye of the Tiger*

# *Chapter 1*

It wasn't that he minded the dinner so much, or the business talk that followed it. What bothered Evan Tremayne was the way Anna sat and watched him.

She was nineteen, blond, buxom and blue-eyed, a statuesque young woman with long tanned legs that looked incredible in shorts. Evan had tried for the past year not to notice her, despite the fact that he and her mother did a lot of business together. At thirty-four, he was the eldest of four brothers, and he had almost total responsibility for their mother. The family business was mostly under his control and his life was one long tangle of cattle, personnel problems and financial headaches. Anna was the last damned straw.

Especially, he thought, in that pale blue dress that showed too much of her golden tan and her full breasts. Surely her mother should have said something about that. He wondered if Polly Cochran noticed how fast her daughter was growing up. Polly was never home, though. She seemed always to be busy with some new facet of her real estate business. Anna's father was an airline pilot, but he and Polly had separated years ago. He lived in Atlanta, Georgia, while they lived in Texas. In fact, Anna had been given most of her upbringing by Lori, the family housekeeper. Nobody seemed to have had much time for her.

Polly had excused herself to take a phone call, and Evan was left uncomfortably alone with Anna.

"Why have you been glowering at me for the past ten minutes?" Anna asked softly. Her blond hair was piled on top of her head, and she looked sophisticated and very mature for a change.

"Because that dress shows too much of you," Evan replied with customary bluntness. His dark eyes glanced from her face to the swell of her breasts. "Polly shouldn't have bought it for you."

"She didn't," Anna said with a grin. "It's one of hers. I borrowed it when she wasn't looking. She hasn't even noticed that I'm wearing it. You know how unobservant she is. Everything with Mama is business."

"Your mother's dresses are too old for you," he replied, softening the words a little with a smile. He tended to be more abrasive with Anna than with anyone else in his life because of his unwanted attraction to her. "You should wear something more appropriate for your own age."

She took a slow breath and her eyes gently worshipped him before they dropped to the table. "Do I really seem so young to you, Evan?"

"I'm thirty-four, little one," he said, his voice deep and slow in the silence of the dining room. "Yes, you seem young."

Her blue eyes settled on her folded hands. "Mama's

giving a party Friday night to celebrate the opening of that new mall in Jacobsville that she sold the property for," she said. "Are you coming?"

"Harden and Miranda might," he murmured. "I stay busy."

She looked up, her eyes searching his dark, broad face relentlessly. "You could dance one dance with me. It wouldn't kill you."

"Wouldn't it?" he asked with graveyard humor. He touched his linen napkin to his wide, chiseled mouth and laid it down beside his plate. He got to his feet, towering over her. He was a giant of a man, all muscle and streamlined, from the broad wedge of his chest to his narrow hips and long, powerful legs. "I have to go."

She stood up. "Not yet," she pleaded.

"I've got things to do," he said.

"No, you haven't," she said, pouting. "You just don't want to be alone with me. What are you afraid of, Evan, that I'll assault you on the table?"

He lifted an eyebrow over twinkling brown eyes. "And get mashed potatoes all over my back?"

She let out an irritated breath. "You won't take me seriously."

"I wouldn't dare," he said, fending her off with the ease of years of practice. "Tell Polly I'll see her tomorrow at the office."

"I could be dying of love for you," she said quietly. "And you don't even care that you're breaking my heart."

He grinned. "Hearts don't break, especially at your age."

"Yes, they do." Her eyes ran up and down his big body, lingering on his broad chest. "You might at least kiss me goodbye."

"Let Randall do that," he replied. "He's still at the experimenting age, like you."

"And you're over the hill, I guess?"

He chuckled. "Feels like it sometimes," he confessed. "Good night, little girl."

She colored delicately, which heightened the blue of her eyes. "I'm not a child!"

"You are to me." He picked up his Stetson from the sideboard without looking at her. "Give my apologies to your mother. I can't wait for her. Thanks for dinner."

Before she could come up with a reply, he was out the door and gone, without even seeming to hurry.

The hell of it was that he was fiercely attracted to her. In fact he could probably fall head over heels in love with her. But she was much too young for a serious relationship. At her age she was likely to fall in and out of love weekly. Besides, she was almost certainly a virgin. Evan was six-four and weighed over two hundred and thirty pounds. A brief love affair had ended in near tragedy because, in his desire for the woman he loved—an innocent woman, like Anna—he hadn't been able to control his great strength. Louisa had run from him, terrified. It had scarred him, made him hopelessly wary of innocents like Anna. His size had been a sore spot with him ever since childhood, when he was forever coming to the defense of his three brothers. He'd always had to pull his punches. He'd even put a man in the hospital once when he'd underestimated his strength. The risk with a sheltered girl like Anna was just too great. No, he couldn't afford another episode like that, he couldn't take the chance. Better to stick to experienced women who weren't afraid of him.

Back at the brick mansion, Anna was raging over the things Evan had said. He was treating her like a teen with a crush, when she was dying of unrequited love for him!

"Where's Evan?" her mother asked, pausing in the

doorway. She was tall and thin and fiftyish, dark, where Anna was fair like her father.

"He left," Anna said curtly. "He was afraid I might bend him over the table and seduce him in the green beans and mashed potatoes."

"What?" Polly asked, laughing.

"He's afraid to be alone with me," Anna muttered. "I suppose he thinks I'll get him pregnant."

"Child, do watch your language," Polly chided. "Never mind Evan. You've already got a beau, much closer to your own age."

Anna sighed. "Good old Randall," she mused. "With the wandering eyes. I like him a lot, but he flirts with every woman he sees. I can't believe he's serious about me."

"He's only in his twenties," Polly said. "Plenty of time to get serious when you're older. Marriage is for the birds, honey."

Anna glared at her. "Just because you and Daddy weren't happy together doesn't mean that I can't have a good marriage."

Polly's eyes darkened and she turned away to light a cigarette, ignoring Anna's disapproving glance as she reached for an ashtray. "Your father and I were very happy at first," her mother corrected. "Then he started flying overseas routes and I got into the real estate business. We never saw each other." She shrugged. "Just one of those things."

"Do you still love him?"

The older woman cocked a perfect dark eyebrow. "Love is a myth."

"Oh, Mama." Anna sighed.

Polly just laughed. "Dream your dreams, child. I'll settle for CDs in the bank and plenty of stocks and bonds in my safety deposit box. Where did you get that dress?"

The younger woman grinned. "It's yours."

Her mother gave her a mock glare. "How many times have I told you to stay out of my closet?"

"Only twenty. You won't buy me anything this sexy."

"I suppose you wore it to tempt Evan," Polly mused. "Well, you might as well give up. Evan's too old for you, and he knows it, even if you don't. Go and change. I'll treat you to a movie."

"Okay."

It was nice to have a mother who was also a good friend, Anna thought as she complied with the request. But nobody seemed inclined to take her feelings for Evan seriously. Especially Evan himself.

Sometimes Anna thought it would be nice if she had a job that would put her in constant contact with Evan. But she couldn't work cattle and she knew nothing about bookkeeping or finance. The best she'd been able to manage was secretarial work at her mother's real estate office. That did bring her into fairly frequent contact with Evan, because the Tremayne brothers were always looking for investment properties. Since Evan was the eldest and headed the company, he was the one her mother saw most frequently. That meant Anna got to see him. She was working on the premise of water dripping on stone. If he was around her enough, he might notice her more.

There were, of course, better ways than just sitting around hoping. Anna had the pursuit of Evan down to a science. She could wrangle invitations to parties he'd attend, she found ways to track him down at lunch and accidentally run into him. She occasionally waylaid him at the post office or the feed store. Most people found her relentless chase amusing, but more and more she sensed that it was affecting Evan. If only he'd just look at her!

It was a well-known fact that Evan hated alcohol. He had

an intense aversion to it for reasons nobody understood. So all Anna had to do to attract his interest at her mother's office the next day was to sit two bottles of unopened whiskey on her desk before he was due at the realty company.

He stopped dead when he saw them, his dark brows knitting over deep-set brown eyes shaded by the brim of the Stetson pulled low over his forehead.

"What the hell is that for?" he demanded, gesturing toward the bottles.

"Medicinal purposes," Anna said smugly. She was wearing a white linen suit with a pink blouse, her hair in a plait, and she looked both businesslike and feminine.

He glared at her. "Try again."

She glanced around to make sure none of the other women in the office were listening, and she leaned forward. "It's to treat snakebite."

The scowl got worse. "There aren't any rattlers in here."

She grinned. "Yes, there are." She pulled open her bottom drawer to reveal two huge plastic snakes with realistic fangs.

Evan's eyes widened. "Good God!"

"These are for people who need an excuse to drink the whiskey."

"Are you out of your mind?"

"If I was, how could I be using it to talk to you?"

He gave up and went past her, shaking his head. Anna watched him, her blue eyes lazily adoring on his tall, powerful body. He was perfectly built, with broad shoulders tapering to slender hips and long legs. He had a rodeo rider's physique, except for his great size. Evan had hands the size of plates. He was even intimidating to some of the women in the office, who made innuendoes that Anna was too sheltered to understand. But Anna found nothing frightening about him at all. She loved him.

He was aware of that silent stare, but he didn't react to it. She was playing games again, he knew it. She had to be aware that the whiskey would draw his attention. It had worked. He had to be more careful from now on, not to fall into her little traps.

But it wasn't that easy. When he came out of Polly's office, Anna wasn't at her desk. He found her outside near his car, on her hands and knees beside the small white Porsche her mother had bought her, looking through a small toolbox.

"Looking for something?" he asked.

"Yes. For my left-handed Johnson wrench."

He sighed impatiently. "There's no such thing."

"There is so. Johnson is the local mechanic and he's left-handed. I borrowed his wrench and now I've lost it."

He threw up his hands. "What's gotten into you today?"

"Maddened passion," she said, standing up, her eyes wide and theatrical, like her audible breathing. "I'm dying for you!" She threw her arms wide and sprawled against the side of the car. "Go ahead, ravish me!"

He was having to choke back laughter. "Where?" he asked, glancing around the big car park.

"On the hood of the car, in the trunk, I don't care!" She was still holding the pose, her eyes closed.

"The hood would break under your weight, never mind mine, and I don't think I could get my head and shoulders in that tiny trunk."

She opened her eyes and glared at him. "On the pavement?"

He shook his head. "Too hard."

"The grass."

"Chiggers and fire ants." He folded his arms over his chest, and his eyes ran down her body slowly and without his usual detachment. In fact, the bold gaze unnerved her. No one, not even Randall, had ever looked at her in that particular glittery way, as if he knew what she looked like with her clothes off.

Defensively, she folded her arms across her jacket. "Don't do that," she said softly.

"You started it, honey," he reminded her, and moved deliberately closer, threatening her with his size and strength. She looked nervous now, which was what he intended. Playing games with grown men could be dangerous. Someone needed to prove it to her.

"Evan…" she said uneasily.

The car park was deserted, and Anna's bravado was quickly disappearing. Flirting was one thing, but she still wasn't quite sure of herself in any intimate situation. She could handle Randall, but Evan had an untamed look about him. He might seem like a big teddy bear at times, but the Tremayne brothers were a fiery bunch and he was the eldest. Probably Connal, Harden and Donald had learned all they knew from his example.

"What's the matter?" he asked with a mocking smile when she backed against the car like a kitten at bay. "Not as safe as you thought?"

She didn't know what she thought anymore. He smelled of cologne and soap, and his height and size were intimidating.

"It's broad daylight," she pointed out.

"I know that." He pursed his wide lips and smiled down at her, but it wasn't any kind of smile she'd ever seen on his lips before. Or on any other man's, come to think of it. It was sensuous and masculine and very arrogant, as if he knew that her knees were weak and her heart was beating her to death.

"I really have to go, Evan," she said, sounding frantic.

He could have pushed it. He almost did. Her very vulnerability attracted him as her blatant flirting never had. His eyes fell to her high, full breasts and narrowed. She was voluptuous in the very best way, well-endowed enough to almost fill hands even the size of his. He started at the direction his thoughts were taking. Anna was a virgin. He reminded himself of that silently and forced his eyes back up to her flushed, stunned face.

"I thought you wanted to get ravished," he said softly, the velvety depth of his voice a threat in itself. "Running away before we even get started?"

She swallowed down her fear and eased away from him, laughing nervously. He made her feel young and totally green. "I'll need to take a lot of vitamins first, to get in shape," she said, glancing at him as she opened the door of her car and climbed in. "Hold that thought, though."

He laughed gently at her grit. She had courage, and she bounced back fast. If she'd been a few years older, anything might happen. "Okay, rabbit, hit the road. But next time, be sure you know what you're asking for," he added, and his eyes were serious. "A man won't usually turn down a blatant invitation, even if it's against his better judgment."

"You've been turning me down for years," she reminded him, catching her breath. "You're experienced."

His dark eyes narrowed on her face. "Yes, I am," he said quietly. "Keep that in mind. You're still at the stage where you think a man's appetite can be satisfied by a few soft kisses. Mine can't."

She glared at him. "I wasn't offering...!"

"Weren't you?"

She averted her gaze to her fingers on the key in the ignition. "No, I wasn't," she said curtly. "I was only teasing."

"That kind of teasing can be dangerous. Practice on Randall. He's safer than I am."

"At least he wants me," she muttered, and she abruptly started the car.

"Good for him," he replied. "Don't speed in that toy car."

She moved the toolbox from the passenger seat to the floorboard. "I never speed," she lied.

He watched her fasten her seat belt. "Through for the day already?" he taunted softly.

"I'm having lunch with my best friend," she said evasively.

He lifted his eyebrows. "I didn't know you had one."

She didn't answer him. She backed out of the parking spot and managed to take off without stripping the gears. Tears glittered in her eyes, but he wouldn't see them.

She stopped at a nearby restaurant and had a hamburger, all by herself. She had no girlfriends. She liked Randall very well. He was a resident at the hospital, the son of the local doctor, and not bad looking. Of course, he did have a wandering eye, but Anna got along with him and didn't feel threatened by him. Her heart was Evan's, sadly enough. How terrible, to love a man who treated you like a child and made fun of you when you offered yourself to him. She could have bawled. Actually, everything was bravado with her, where Evan was concerned. She'd teased him just to get his attention. But having gotten it, she didn't know what to do with it. He was experienced, and she wasn't. She didn't know how to handle a man like that. She'd just been shown graphically that she was totally out of her element with Evan.

She went back to the office late, and her heart wasn't in her work for the rest of the day. Polly didn't even notice. Anna wondered sometimes if her mother paid much attention to anything that she didn't want to see.

The party her mother gave to celebrate the opening of the new Jacobsville mall gave Anna an excuse to dress to the back teeth. Not, she told herself, that Evan was going to notice. He'd already said he probably wouldn't come. Randall would be there, though. She could certainly dress up for him.

She wore a witchy, silver, crystal-pleated dress that fell in layers to just below her knees. She let her blond hair waft loosely around her shoulders, straight and heavy, and she wore sexy little high-heeled sandals on her feet. She knew she looked good, but the evening felt flat. She added a hint of pastel lipstick to her full lips and brushed her hair, but her heart wasn't in her preparations. Without Evan, her whole life was flat and uninteresting.

Downstairs Randall was waiting for her, looking very trendy in his sports coat and neatly pressed slacks. He wore wire-rimmed glasses, and he was very dignified. Not a hair out of place, although what he had was thinning above his forehead. He wasn't handsome. But women loved him. He had a gentle, caring demeanor and he was good company, even if he did have the worst kind of wandering eye. Anna liked him, and the feeling was mutual.

"You look very nice," he told her, glancing around at the very elegant crowd Polly was entertaining. "Your mother knows everybody, doesn't she?"

"Everyone who moves in her circles," Anna replied. Randall's interest in the wealthy set disturbed her. Anna had never mixed with people simply because of their wealth or social status. Neither did the Tremaynes. Randall was thinking ahead to the time when he would be in practice, she was sure. His preference for an uptown medical practice was something he made no secret of.

He took Anna's arm and guided her through to the canapé table, where ruby punch and savories were being offered to the guests. "I'm starved. I had to forego lunch for exams. I wish this was a sit-down affair."

"Lori did honey chicken and salmon croquettes," she told him, gesturing toward platters of food. "And there are little blueberry muffins, too. If you load enough on your plate, you'll get full."

He smiled at her. "I guess so."

She noticed the couples moving to the soft music of the live band. She loved to dance, but Randall couldn't. He had no desire to learn, even though she'd offered to teach him.

"You wouldn't like to shuffle around the floor?" she tried yet once more.

He shook his head. "Sorry. I'm tired. I want to get off my feet, not on them!"

She lifted her shoulders as if she didn't care. She got a cup of punch, looking around for familiar faces. When she spotted Harden and Miranda Tremayne, her eyes went helplessly past them, hoping for a glimpse of Evan. But he wasn't there. Her face fell, even as she smiled a greeting at the couple.

Miranda was wearing a black maternity dress with flowing lace, and she had a radiant Harden beside her. Anna had always felt a little sorry for Harden, because he'd seemed so alone. But these days, he smiled a lot, and the old coldness was gone from his blue eyes.

He had a possessive arm around Miranda's swollen waist, and he looked devastating in a dinner jacket. Almost, Anna thought, as good as Evan looked similarly clothed.

"Nice turnout," Harden murmured dryly. "Your mother outdid herself."

"Indeed she did," Anna said, grinning. "Do I get introduced? I've seen Miranda, but I've never actually gotten to meet her."

"Miranda, this is Anna Cochran," Harden obliged. "You met Polly at the Chamber of Commerce banquet a few days ago. Polly sold the property for the new mall and helped coax in some new businesses."

"I'm very glad to meet you," Miranda said, smiling back, her silvery eyes almost the color of Anna's dress. "I've heard a lot about you."

Anna sighed. "About my relentless pursuit of Evan, I guess," she murmured ruefully. "It's a hopeless cause, but I can't seem to get out of the habit. One day he'll marry somebody and I can give up with good grace."

"That doesn't seem likely," Harden replied on a sigh. "Evan is sure he's doomed to perpetual bachelorhood. He's forever moaning that women won't give him the time of day."

"His excuse used to be that they trampled him trying to get to Harden." Miranda laughed, swinging her long, dark hair. "Nowadays, he's convinced that he's too old to appeal to anyone."

"Thirty-four and ready for 'the home,'" Harden agreed. He shook his head. "Save him, Anna."

"I'm trying," she laughed. "But he won't let me put away my baby dolls and my play tea set. He thinks I'm a mere child."

"He wouldn't if he saw you in that dress," Miranda said with a conspiratory smile. "You look very elegant."

"At least Randall noticed," Anna grimaced. "Want to meet him?"

She turned to drag Randall over by one arm while he

nibbled on chicken wings. "This is Randall Wayne," she told them. "He's a medical student."

"I'm a resident, thank you very much," Randall said, glowering at her. "Only a short leap from my own practice, when I finish my residency next year," he added, grinning at them. "Remember me if you break anything."

"I'll do that," Harden promised.

"Oh, Randall." Anna sighed. "You're hopeless."

"Patients are scarce for young doctors," he reminded her. "Can't blame a man for trying to drum up business in advance."

"Certainly not," Miranda said laughing.

Anna didn't want to ask, but she couldn't quite help it. "I don't suppose any of the rest of the family came with you?" she asked.

"Just Evan," Harden murmured reluctantly, watching the way her eyes brightened. "He's parking the car." He didn't want to tell her the rest. Anna's helpless attraction to Evan was so obvious that he was already hurting for her.

"He may be out there all night," Randall pointed out. "It took me thirty minutes to find someplace to leave my car."

"Evan's resourceful," Harden said. He glanced regretfully at Anna. She was going to need time to steel herself before Evan came in. He owed her that. "And Nina's with him. She's a whiz at finding the impossible."

## Chapter 2

Anna didn't know how she managed to respond to that casual comment, but she saved her pride with a smile and an offhand remark. Evan had made it abundantly clear that he didn't want her adulation, now he was pushing the knife home. He'd brought Nina, whom everyone knew was his old flame. The woman was now a successful fashion model in Houston, and she was visiting locally. Probably she was doing her best to rekindle those embers. If Evan had brought her to Polly's party, he had to be encouraging her.

"My brother is an idiot," Harden told Miranda as they moved away, his blue eyes glittering. "My God, did you see what it did to her? Evan thinks she's a child, but the kind of hurt I saw in her face isn't juvenile."

"Doesn't he feel anything at all for her?" Miranda asked.

"I don't know. If he does, he's buried it. He's stubborn,

and he can be cruel when he's pushed. Anna's made a game of it, playing at flirting and teasing. He thinks that's all there is to it. He doesn't think she's serious."

"But she is."

He nodded. "I'm sure of it. It's a camouflage. After all, the safest way to hide your feelings is to exaggerate them. Poor little thing. Randall isn't a patch on Evan, but she'll wind up marrying him out of unrequited love for my brother."

"Such a waste." Miranda sighed.

He pulled her closer. "Indeed, it is. Thank God we're past all that uncertainty."

She smiled, lifting radiant eyes to his. "I love you."

His blue eyes kindled. He bent and kissed her softly. "I can send that back, multiplied."

"Yes," she whispered, pressing close. "I know. We have so much, Harden."

His lean hand lightly touched the soft swell of her belly and his eyes blazed into hers. "More than I ever dreamed," he whispered. "Did I ever tell you that you're my life?"

Miranda was too choked with emotion to even answer. She pressed close against his side while his lips brushed her forehead with exquisite tenderness.

Anna, watching them covertly, wanted to cry. What they felt for each other was almost tangible. She'd never known that kind of intimate caring. She probably never would. Randall's idea of romance was a few kisses punctuated with groping. He might make an excellent doctor, but he had a long way to go as even a lukewarm lover. And he wasn't, could never be, Evan.

She sipped her punch while Randall spoke to someone he knew from the hospital. She wouldn't look at the door, she absolutely wouldn't. She wasn't going to give Evan the satisfaction of knowing that he was killing her with his indifference.

"Finally, something to drink!" came a husky, purring voice from behind her. "Hello, Anna!" Nina Ray said, smiling faintly. "I hope that punch is spiked. I really need a drink. Evan had to park almost in the pond! My feet are killing me from so much walking."

"That's nothing unusual is it, for a model?" Evan taunted.

Anna couldn't meet his eyes. She glanced at his white shirt and black tie and dinner jacket and averted her gaze to gorgeously dark Nina in a white and black gown that put everyone else's dresses to shame.

"You look great," Anna said sincerely. "I see you all the time in fashion magazines. For a small-town girl, you sure hit it big."

"I had a lot of help, lovey," Nina mused. She glanced up at Evan with a self-confident sexiness that made Anna grind her teeth in frustration. She'd never learn how to do that.

"Where's Polly?" Evan asked as he filled punch cups for Nina and then himself.

"Circulating," Anna said, smiling. "She's very much the lady of the hour."

"She deserves it," Evan replied. "That mall will bring in a lot of new businesses, and plenty of revenue."

"Everything helps to swell the tax base," Randall remarked, joining them. He smiled at Nina. "You look lovely!" he enthused, and Anna could have hit him. He hadn't been half that vocal about her own appearance.

"Thank you. And who's this?" Nina asked, her dark eyes flirting with Randall.

"Randall Wayne," he said, taking her slender hand in

his. He actually kissed the knuckles, just above the red-painted nails. "Nice to meet you, Miss Ray."

Nina beamed. "You know who I am?"

"Everyone does. Your face is unmistakable. I see it on magazine covers all the time."

"Yes." Nina sighed complacently. "My career has taken off since Evan helped me find that new agency."

"Anything to help," Evan said suavely. He was trying not to notice Anna and failing miserably. In that silver gown, her exquisite skin was displayed almost too blatantly. Her honey-brown tan made her complexion even prettier and emphasized her big blue eyes. It was an effort to keep away from her.

"The band is very good," Nina remarked. "Evan, do let's dance!"

She took his hand and headed for the dance floor without giving him time to speak to Randall or Anna. Not that he would have, anyway, Anna thought. He was giving her a blatant message—hands off. She lifted her cup of punch to her lips with a sigh.

"This punch needs help," one of the guests remarked, slipping a bottle of whiskey from under his dinner jacket. "Here goes!"

Anna watched him fill the bowl with a wry grin. She knew one of the guests would have hives if he saw that. Evan didn't like punch, though, so there was little likelihood that he'd imbibe. He hated alcohol. Anna had heard that he actually took a glass of wine back to the kitchen one night when he was having dinner with Justin and Shelby Ballenger.

She mentioned that to Randall after the punch spiker had sampled his handiwork and retired to the dance floor with his partner.

"Yes, I heard about that," Randall remarked. "Justin and Shelby have three boys now, haven't they?"

"Yes. They're neck and neck with Calhoun and Abby."

"They have two boys and a girl," he reminded her. "I heard Harden and Evan's brother Connal mention it at a party I attended a week ago."

She laughed gently. "Connal insisted that Calhoun and Abby had a daughter just after their second child was born. They don't. They have a son named Terry, and when Connal heard the name, he assumed they'd gotten the daughter they wanted. He knows better now, of course, but it's become something of a family joke. Not that anybody mentions it to Calhoun or Abby."

"Terry is kind of a unisex name," Randall said.

"It's short for Terrance, which isn't," she corrected. "Imagine that—two brothers and six sons and not a girl in the bunch." She shook her head.

"What about Shelby's brother, Tyler?"

"He and his wife can't have children," Anna said with quiet regret. "But they've adopted five! Nell was very upset, but Tyler involved her in one of those foster parent programs. In no time, she was knee-deep in kids who'd had no real home at all. They said the children are the greatest miracle of their lives."

"A unique solution," Randall agreed. "One couple in seven is infertile. It must be difficult, although they seem to have found a way to cope with the loss."

Anna lowered her eyes to the punch table and thought about never having Evan's children. Not that she would, because he had Nina. It was sad and sobering.

"I suppose if you love each other, no obstacle is insurmountable," she said dimly.

"I suppose. Here. Try some of this. It's rather good."

He handed her a cup of spiked punch and she sipped it,

wincing at the sting of the alcohol on her tongue. The ice fruit ring hadn't diluted the whiskey very much, and Anna seldom drank.

"That's strong stuff," she remarked.

"Only if you aren't used to it." He chuckled. "You're just like Evan about alcohol, aren't you?"

She averted her face. He obviously had no idea how much that remark hurt her. "I don't like alcohol," she said absently.

"Yes, I've noticed."

She didn't hear the faint mockery in his tone. Her eyes had been drawn against her will to Evan. He was so tall and husky that he dwarfed almost every other man in the room. He had the lovely Nina close in his big arms and he was holding her with casual intimacy. Both her slender arms were looped around his neck; his hands on her waist held her carelessly close. He'd never held Anna like that. Probably he never would.

Her eyes softened and saddened at the sight of him. In evening clothes, he was devastating. His dark tan was emphasized by the white shirt he wore, and the black tie, dinner jacket and slacks made him look taller and very dignified. Just looking at him made Anna feel warm and safe, like coming home. If only he felt that way about her. It would be heaven.

Evan felt her rapt gaze and met it across the room. It was like lightning striking. His body tautened helplessly, and his eyes narrowed. Anna again, he thought angrily, playing with matches. She didn't know what she was doing. At nineteen she was just beginning to feel her power as a woman, and she was using it blatantly with every man who came close to her. That was all it was, so he'd better remember.

He tore his gaze away and bent to kiss Nina in front of

the whole assembly. He did it thoroughly and with fierce need, to banish the sight of Anna's wounded face.

Nina was breathless when he let her go, and Anna had vanished. At least he'd accomplished that much.

"Want to take me home right now, big man?" Nina asked huskily. "I'm willing."

But Evan wasn't. He shook his head. "We'd better not vanish before Polly makes her speech," he said with forced humor.

Nina sighed. "You still don't really want me, do you?" she asked quietly. "I can't get you within a mile of my apartment."

"We're friends," he reminded her, smiling. "Otherwise, why would I be giving your career a helping hand?"

"To make some other woman jealous, I'm beginning to think," she said candidly, watching his eyelids flinch. "Or to use me as camouflage. Because you certainly don't want me just for myself. You hardly ever take me out."

He smiled. "I keep busy."

"Not that busy, and you don't go out with many women. That's right—" she nodded when she saw his puzzled expression "—I still have friends in Jacobsville who keep me up-to-date on who's seeing whom. You don't date anyone regularly. The gossip is that Anna Cochran has been seen pursuing you everywhere except up a tree."

He drew in a heavy breath. "That's partially true."

"So that's why you brought me here. Probably why you kissed me, too." She smiled lazily. "Okay, lover. If you need protection, here I am. Do your worst. We'll say it's for old times' sake."

"You're very generous," he mused.

"You've been that," she replied seriously. "I'll help you scrape the kid off, no problem."

He didn't like it put that way, as if Anna was a leech. He frowned.

"She's a babe in the woods, isn't she?" Nina was saying, her eyes on Anna standing at the punch bowl with Randall. "Is she going to marry the medical student, do you think?"

"How should I know?" he asked irritably. He'd never thought of Randall as much of a threat to Anna's maidenhood, but she was spending a lot of time with the younger man lately.

"She's well-to-do. Or her mother is," Nina mused, thinking aloud. "A young doctor going into practice needs a rich wife."

Evan stiffened. "Anna isn't that stupid."

"Darling, she's a teenager. What does she know about men? My God, I'll bet she's even a virgin!"

Evan didn't want to think about that. It made his blood run hot. He turned Nina to the rhythm. "Anna is Randall's business, not mine. Dance. Help me get her off my neck."

Nina smiled warmly. "My pleasure."

Anna watched them dance and took another sip of her punch, and then another. "I wish you could dance, Randall," she said, the words sounding a little slurred. She felt very relaxed.

"So do I, sometimes. Want to try it?" he asked, putting down his cup. "I feel pretty loose right now."

"Good."

She went into his arms and taught him the basic two-step. He began to grin, and his hands brought her gently closer.

"This is nice," he said wonderingly.

"So it is." She lay her cheek on his chest and closed her eyes, barely moving as the music continued. The devil with

Evan, she told herself. She didn't care if he made love to his old flame right there on the dance floor. She just wouldn't look.

"Having a good time, Anna?" one of Polly's friends asked as she danced nearby with her husband.

"Oh, yes," Anna replied politely. "I hope you are."

"It's lovely. Evan's brought someone with him, I see," the woman added with a faintly mocking smile. "Warding you off, is he?"

Anna flushed. Over the years she'd gotten used to being teased about her pursuit of Evan, but tonight it stung. "Nina's an old friend of his," she pointed out.

"Yes, but he doesn't usually come to Polly's parties with a woman in tow. In fact," she said cattily, "he doesn't usually come at all these days, does he? I suppose he's really desperate if he has to look up old flames to discourage you."

Anna pulled away from Randall, who was openly scowling, and moved back to the punch bowl, leaving the woman with her mouth open.

"What are you so upset about?" Randall asked, joining her there. "Everybody knows that you used to chase Evan. You're not doing it now, so why let people bother you?" He slid an arm around her waist. "You've got me, now."

Had she really? Every time a new woman came into the room, she could see Randall's eyes sizing her up. He was a born flirt, and despite his lack of conventional good looks, he could be utterly charming.

"I guess I didn't realize how blatant I must have seemed," Anna said quietly, her eyes downcast. "I was only playing." She hadn't been, but it salvaged some of her pride to pretend she was.

"I know that," Randall said. "So do most other people. Don't worry about gossip. I've been ignoring it for weeks."

Her head jerked up. "What have you heard?"

He shrugged and smiled a little. "Just that you'd been madly pursuing Evan all over town. Accidental meetings that weren't accidental, hanging around him at parties and flirting shamelessly, that kind of thing. They said Evan couldn't go anywhere in Jacobsville without your turning up there. I thought it was funny."

"Evan didn't," she said miserably. "I went overboard and he's finally reached the end of his rope. I wish I'd realized sooner how silly I was behaving."

"Was that woman right? Did he bring the lovely Nina to ward you off?"

She nodded, feeling conspicuous now. "I'm sure of it. Poor Evan."

"I don't know," Randall murmured, smiling at her. "It must be flattering to be chased by a pretty young woman."

"It must be exasperating, you mean," she said, suddenly understanding. How could she have let things go that far without realizing the position she was putting Evan in? She'd teased and flirted, hoping to make him notice her. But all she'd accomplished was to scare him off. What an idiot she'd been!

As if realizing that wasn't bad enough, she had to face the fact that everyone knew that his squiring of Nina was to keep her at bay. It was humiliating to have him publicly reject her like this. As she glanced around, she caught people looking at her and began to notice the faint pity in their eyes.

She had to fight tears as the evening wore on. Evan danced with no one except Nina and was so attentive to her that speculation on the rekindling of the old relationship ran rampant. The way he avoided Anna spoke volumes.

Nobody noticed that Anna was doing her best to avoid him as well. She clung to Randall like a leech.

Polly gave a speech and introduced two of the mall's main backers, along with the merchants who were already committed to opening businesses in it. The speech was well received, and it did divert Anna from her misery.

But despite Randall's company, Anna felt dejected and empty inside. She put on a good front, laughing and glittering, so that no one would guess how badly hurt she was.

When the crowd started to dwindle, Polly paused beside her daughter with an affectionate smile. "I thought it went rather well. How are you doing, darling?"

"Marvelous, thanks," Anna said airily, forcing a smile. "It's been lovely, hasn't it, Randall?"

Randall was watching her narrowly. "How many times have you hit that punch bowl, Anna?"

"Only three," she said, blinking. "Why?"

He exchanged a knowing look with Polly.

"Somebody spiked the punch," Polly guessed.

"How did you know?"

"Evan smelled his punch and put it down with a vicious glare in my direction," Polly said dryly.

"I should have known he'd notice it first." Randall laughed. He checked his watch. "Goodness, I've got to go. I'm on call at the hospital from midnight, and it's almost that. I'll be in touch tomorrow or the next day, as soon as I get some free time. 'Night," he murmured, brushing a careless kiss across Anna's forehead.

She watched him go with no real interest. Polly put an affectionate arm around her shoulders.

"It's killing you, isn't it?" she asked with unusual protectiveness. "You'll survive, my darling. We all do. Evan just isn't the type to settle down. You've always known that."

"I was only ever flirting," Anna said stubbornly. "It wasn't for real. I thought he knew it."

Polly didn't contradict her daughter. She recognized the anguish in those blue eyes, though. Her arm contracted. "Let's go and listen to the band. Randall will phone tomorrow. Maybe he'll take you out to eat. You stay home too much."

"I guess I do. Randall's nice."

"You'll learn one day that we have to take what we can get out of life and not wish for the impossible things too hard," Polly said gently. "One day at a time, pet."

Anna smiled. "Yes." But she was thinking of how many days it was going to take to get over tonight.

Evan and Nina gravitated toward them, and Anna had to fight the urge to cut and run.

"It was a lovely party. Thank you for asking me," Nina said with a smile in Polly's direction.

"It was my pleasure," the older woman replied. "Evan, I'm glad you came, too. I didn't really expect you. If Nina managed to pry you out of your office, good for her."

"I plan to pry him out a lot more often, now," Nina purred, leaning against Evan's shoulder. Anna didn't speak or look at him, and after a minute, he stared at her openly.

"How much of that punch have you had?" Evan demanded of Anna, his dark eyes sparking.

She didn't look at him. "Only a little," she lied. "I know it's spiked."

"You should have poured it out and made more," he told Polly bluntly. "Anna isn't allowed to drink hard liquor, surely?"

Polly started. "Evan, she's nineteen, going on twenty," she said with urbane amusement. "Of course she's allowed to drink."

"Alcohol can kill," he persisted. "Especially if she ever gets in the habit of driving under the influence. She could go to jail…"

"I don't drink and drive, Evan," Anna said solemnly. "I never would. If the alcohol bothers you so much, why don't you go home?"

She poured herself another cup—her fourth, actually—and lifted it to her lips, draining it while her blue eyes defied the angry dark ones glaring at her.

"Can't you do anything with her?" he demanded of Polly.

Anna's eyebrows arched. "My mother doesn't tell me what to do anymore."

Evan's own eyebrows arched. That didn't sound like Anna. Not at all. "You're not used to liquor," he began.

She smiled coldly. "Watch me get used to it," she replied, still smarting from his public humiliation of her and wanting to hurt back. "Nothing I do is any of your damned business. You remember that."

She whirled on her heel, a little wobbly, and went toward the staircase. The whiskey in the punch was lying heavily on her stomach and she felt nausea rising in her throat. But she felt as if she'd just declared independence, and it wasn't a bad feeling at all. Evan wasn't going to be her fatal weakness anymore. Even if she'd deserved his rejection, he could have simply spoken to her in private. He didn't have to do it like this.

Evan stared after her, scowling. It was the first time in memory that Anna had talked back to him. He was used to blind adoration from her, or at worst, pert, flirting comments. Stark hostility was new and all too exciting. His body was reacting to her antagonism in ways he'd never expected.

"She's a bit tipsy, I think, Evan. Don't mind anything

she says," Polly said, waving it off. "By the way, I've got a new investment property that you might be interested in. Want to stop by the office sometime next week and look over a prospectus?"

"Yes, I'd like that," Evan said, preoccupied.

"Let's go," Nina coaxed. "I'm so tired, and I've got a show in the morning."

"Sure. Good night, Polly," Evan said.

She nodded, smiling curiously at the way Evan's eyes kept going to the staircase. His possessive attitude toward Anna startled and amused her. Of course, Evan was thirty-four, too old to be taking any real masculine interest in her poor, lovesick daughter. She turned and went back to her remaining guests, thrusting his odd behavior to the back of her mind. Anna would get over him. It was just a crush.

Anna was sick most of the night, and not just from the alcohol. It had been an eye-opening experience to have Evan flaunt a woman in front of her. For all of the two years, she'd been madly pursuing him, he'd never used that counterattack before. Probably now that he knew it bothered her, it wouldn't be the last time he resorted to it.

Well, she told herself, that was that. If he was desperate enough to throw himself into the arms of an old flame to escape Anna, it was time to retreat. She'd always known somehow that he was never going to take her seriously. She should have given up long ago.

The next morning she braided her long blond hair, put on her shorts and halter top and went out to set up her easel in the garden. She loved to paint. She was quite good at landscapes, having even sold a few. It gave her something to do when she wasn't working.

Polly was at the office today—she sometimes worked seven days a week. But Anna worked five and painted the other two. Now she was toying seriously with the idea of quitting the office. She loved art and she had an eye for investment paintings. She could ask the owner of the local art gallery, who was a friend of the family, to give her a job. It would get her away from the office, where she was all too likely to run into Evan. He wanted her out of his life, so she decided that she'd give him a helping hand. It was the least she could do after having pestered him for two years. Cold sober, she could even understand why he'd brought Nina to the party last night. Poor man. He must have been at the very end of his rope.

As she dabbed paint on the canvas, she considered her options. She didn't really want to leave home, but even that might be a good idea. She was going on twenty years old. It was time she had a life of her own, apart from her mother's. She had to start thinking about her future. Marrying Randall was hardly an option, even though he'd been hinting that he wouldn't be averse to the idea. Considering Polly's wealth, it would be a strategic move on his part. It would give him the financial wherewithal to buy into an established practice, because certainly Polly would be willing to help her new son-in-law.

The landscape she was working on was a study of sunflowers against the sky. She was using a huge sunflower in the garden as a model. It was a lazy summer day with only a slight breeze, and the sun felt like heaven on her skin.

A car door slammed. She didn't look up. It was almost lunchtime and she was expecting her mother.

"I'm out back," she called. "If you're ready, there's a pasta salad in the fridge. I want to finish this before I come in."

Footsteps answered her shout, but they didn't belong to a woman. They were too heavy.

Her head turned just as Evan came around the side of

the house. He was wearing work clothes—jeans and a dust-stained blue plaid shirt, with disreputable boots and a Stetson that was battered almost beyond recognition. She stiffened with hurt indignation, but she couldn't afford to let it show. She turned back to her painting.

"Where's Polly?" he asked without preamble.

So much for the forlorn hope that he might have come to see her, to apologize for dragging her pride through the dust the night before. She kept her eyes on the canvas, so that he wouldn't see the disappointment in them.

"If she isn't at the office, she's on her way here for lunch, I guess," she said.

His dark eyes slid over her with reluctant interest. "She was supposed to leave a prospectus for me on a new piece of land. Know anything about it?"

She shook her head. "Sorry." She traced a sunflower petal with maniacal accuracy, to keep her mind off her breaking heart. "If you'd like to wait, Lori can make you some iced tea."

Anna was so unlike her usual self that he felt out of his element. "What? No invitation to ravish you among the sunflowers?"

"I've decided to grow up," she said without looking at him. "Chasing after unwilling men is for adolescents. From now on, I'm only going after men I think I can catch."

"Like Randall?" he asked.

She shrugged. "Why not?"

Her attitude disturbed him. He leaned against the fence that surrounded the small garden. "I didn't know you painted."

"At the speed you always go around me, I'm not surprised," she said imperturbably and dotted more yellow on the canvas. "No more games, Evan," she said, looking up at him quietly. "I got the message last night. If you really came here to make it clear, there's no need." She managed a smile. "I'm sorry I made your life so difficult. I won't embarrass you anymore, I promise."

He felt empty. His eyes narrowed as she turned back to her canvas. She didn't sound like herself. In fact, he mused, she didn't look like the kid he'd always thought her. Those long, tanned legs were a woman's, like the full breasts under that skimpy halter. She was delectable.

He quietly watched her. "Are you and Polly going to the Ballenger barbecue next week?"

"I don't know." She glanced at him shyly. "If you're going to be there, probably not. I don't want to do your social life any more damage than I already have. No wonder you've been staying away from local social occasions. I had no idea how difficult I'd made things for you until the gossip started to get back to me."

He started. That didn't sound like Anna. He opened his mouth to speak, but before he could deny the insinuation, Polly's car roared up the driveway. Seconds later she came around the corner, having seen Evan's car. "There you are!" she said, laughing. "I've brought the prospectus. I was going to run it out to you. Anna, is lunch ready?"

"Lori said it's on the table," Anna replied. "I'll be in later. I want to finish this while the light's right."

"Artists." Polly sighed. "Okay, honey. Evan, stay and eat with me, since Anna's bent on being eccentric."

Evan's dark eyes lingered on Anna's profile. "I have to get back to work myself," he said hesitantly. "We're moving in new cattle today, so everybody's out in the yards helping—even mother."

"In a few years, you'll have plenty of help," Polly laughed. "All those babies coming along."

"Yes." He turned and took the prospectus Polly was

holding out. "I'll run through this with Harden and the others and give you a call when we decide."

"Fine. Sure you won't stay for lunch?"

He waited for Anna to say something, to second her mother's offer at least. But she didn't. She said nothing. She didn't look up. After a minute, he shrugged and made his excuses.

When he was gone, Polly considered her daughter with open curiosity.

"Have you and Evan argued?" she asked softly.

"Of course not," Anna said. She turned, smiling, to her mother. "I've just decided to stop making his life miserable. Having me dog him at every step must have been wearing."

Polly relaxed a little. "I'm sure he realizes it's just a stage you're going through, darling," she replied gently. "Evan's not a bad man. He's just a card-carrying bachelor. You're a marrying type of girl. Even if you weren't years too young for him your goals are too different."

"You're right, of course," Anna said, trying not to choke on the words.

"I imagine he'll be pleased to be off the endangered list, all the same." She laughed. "You were getting pretty relentless. I, uh, heard about the whiskey bottles and the plastic snakes."

"Another ploy in my relentless campaign that failed." Anna sighed, managing not to reveal how hurt she really was. She concentrated on her canvas. "Well, it's over now. He did look relieved, didn't he?"

Polly nodded, but her eyes were saying something else. She wasn't sure exactly how Evan had looked, but relief wasn't the word she would have chosen. She had the oddest feeling that Anna had shocked him.

## Chapter 3

In fact, *perplexed* was more the way Evan felt as he drove back to the Tremayne ranch. He hadn't slept well, remembering the way Anna had looked when he and Nina left the party. He'd used the prospectus as an excuse to come over and see how much damage he'd done.

What he'd found had surprised him. Anna was apparently indifferent to his presence and not at all anxious for his company. After two years of being pursued, teased, flirted with and vamped, it was shocking to have Anna treat him like a stranger.

He pulled up at the house and went inside, scowling.

"Something bothering you?" Harden asked from the study doorway.

Evan went in and closed the door. He could talk to Harden as he could to no one else, and he needed a sympathetic ear right now.

"Anna's bothering me," he said shortly.

"That's nothing new," Harden replied. "You've been complaining about Anna for as long as I can remember."

Evan scowled, turning. "No," he said. "You don't understand. She's ignoring me."

Harden's blue eyes twinkled. "A new ploy?"

Evan sat perched on the edge of the desk. "She hasn't been the same since last night. She's decided that she's been ruining my life, so she's giving me up."

"Nice of her," Harden commented.

"It's the way she's doing it that worries me," came the quiet reply. "She's too calm."

"You didn't see the way she looked when she saw you with Nina," Harden replied. "It cut her up."

Evan cursed under his breath. "I thought I was doing the right thing. I didn't want to hurt her. I just wanted to get her off my back."

"You did. So what's the problem?"

The bigger man sighed wearily. "I didn't know how it was going to feel, having her ignore me completely."

"Quite an admission from you, isn't it?"

"I guess it is." He studied his worn boot. "But I still think I did the right thing. She's years too young."

"So you keep saying. I guess she finally listened."

"I guess."

"Nina seems smitten all over again. Is it serious?"

Evan's dark eyes met his brother's blue ones. "I don't want Nina. That was over years ago. I financed some new publicity for her and she's paying me back."

"I see," Harden murmured. "She's helping you fend off Anna."

"Unnecessarily, as it happens. Anna's dropped her mad pursuit. She said the game was over. Was that what it was all along to her—a game?"

"Maybe you're the one who was taking it too seriously," Harden said gently. "Anna played with you, brought you out of your shell. There were times when you almost seemed to enjoy it. Then you'd get your back up and complain that she was hounding you."

True enough, Evan thought, because just occasionally he felt a raging desire for Anna that he had to quell. It had been building for a long time, but lately it was explosive. Nina had been an act of desperation, as Anna had said. But the action seemed to be backfiring. He was the one who'd been burned.

"Anna's a virgin," Evan said shortly. "I'm almost certain of it. I had a rough experience with an innocent woman. These days, I look for sophistication."

"I know that," Harden replied kindly. "But that woman wasn't Anna. If she loved you, really loved you…"

"Anna isn't old enough to be that serious about a man."

"I hope you're right," he murmured. "Because if she really cared, and you've killed it, you may have cost yourself the brightest star in your sky."

Evan scowled. "I told you, she said it was only a game!"

"Would she be likely to confess undying love when you'd just thrown one of your old conquests in her face?"

Of course not. This was getting him nowhere. "I'll get back out to the stockyard. Coming?"

"In a minute. I've got to drive Miranda in to the doctor," he said, grinning.

Evan shook his head. "First Pepi, now Miranda and Jo Anne. I'm surrounded by pregnant women."

"Uncle Evan," Harden mocked.

The big man smiled gently. "I love kids. I guess it's going to be up to mother and me to spoil them all."

"You might have some of your own one day."

Evan's eyes grew quiet and sad. "That isn't on the books."

"Anna's not afraid of you, for God's sake!" Harden growled.

"Of course she isn't, I've never made a heavy pass at her!" Evan replied levelly, his dark eyes unblinking. "Louisa was fine until I tried to take her to bed!"

Harden stared at him. "Nothing ventured, nothing gained."

"Even if Anna was old enough, I'd never have the nerve, don't you see?" He stuck his hands in his pockets and stared out the window. "That one experience spoiled intimacy for me. I lost control and hurt Louisa. I've been afraid ever since that I'd do it again. I put Randy Hardy in the hospital when we got into that brawl a few years back, didn't I?" he added to emphasize his concern.

"Accidentally."

"Yes. Well, I could do the same thing to a woman if I lost my head," Evan returned hotly. "My size is no joke."

"You're big," Harden agreed. "And strong as a bull. Nobody's arguing with that. But you're giving yourself a complex, and it's not necessary. Just because one hysterical woman accused you of breaking her ribs…"

"I did bruise them pretty badly," Evan said miserably.

"She bruised them by trying to fight you and falling out of bed," Harden reminded him harshly. "She was half your size and all bones, and a terrified virgin into the bargain. Anna is a big girl, tall and sturdy and voluptuous. She's much more your type."

"I don't want Anna!" Evan returned.

"Suit yourself. She'll probably marry the honorable physician and have ten kids."

"If that's what she wants." His blood ran cold at the

thought of Randall giving her children. He stuck his hat over his eyes and walked out of the room.

Harden, watching him, shook his head. He couldn't talk to Evan anymore. The older man was running scared, even if he wouldn't admit it. If he wasn't careful, he was going to make a mess of not only his life, but Anna's as well.

In the days that followed, Evan noticed a difference in his life. He went to town, and there was no more Anna peering over his shoulder in the hardware store or peeking out of her mother's office window to grin and wave at him. He went to a local social gathering, and Anna hadn't begged an invitation so that she could flirt with him. He took the precaution of taking Nina with him, just in case, but it hadn't been necessary.

He should have been jubilant, but somehow it wounded him that Anna didn't want him anymore. All his arguments against the relationship didn't help.

Two weeks after the party, Anna was shopping at the local boutique when Nina danced in, wafting expensive perfume and looking on top of the world.

"Well, hello!" she greeted Anna, smiling. "So Evan did finally beat you off! We didn't see a sign of you at the Andersons' get-together night before last! He spent the first few minutes peeking around corners in case you showed up. You really gave him a complex."

Anna felt sick at the way Nina had put it. "Yes. Well, I'm devoting myself to Randall these days."

"The doctor with the wandering eye, hmm?" Nina mused, fingering one of the more expensive dresses in the shop. "He won't be easy to hold, I'm afraid. I don't suppose you know he took Cindy Grayson to the swimming party at the Fords' Monday? Or that she didn't get home until daylight?"

Anna glared at the older woman. "Is all this malice really necessary? You've got Evan. What more do you want?"

Nina's delicate eyebrows levered up. "I haven't 'got' Evan at all," she said. "He only asked me out to keep you away from him. He said he'd do anything to scrape you off." Her eyes darkened as they studied Anna haughtily. "You should have known that his type of man doesn't like being chased. You cut your own throat."

"Well, he's safe now," Anna said, almost choking.

Nina shrugged. "I doubt he'll believe it. Not that I mind," she added cattily. "Because the longer he feels you're a threat, the longer I'll have with him. He's quite something in bed," she said deliberately, watching Anna blush.

Anna left the dress she was looking at and went out the door of the boutique as if her jeans were on fire. Nina watched her for a minute and then turned back to the dress racks. That had been easy enough. She didn't like the way Evan was preoccupied since Anna's defection. Only if Anna was kept away would Nina have a clear shot at Evan. The fiction of sleeping with him seemed to do the trick, though. She was actually humming by the time she left the shop.

For the rest of the afternoon Anna barely knew what was going on around her. She left early and went to the Taylor Gallery.

Brand Taylor was elderly, with a keen eye for art and a thorough knowledge of the market for it. He'd known Anna since she was a child, and he'd followed her interest in art with pleasure.

"I've been hoping you might approach me for a job one day," he told her honestly when she asked about it. "I'm here alone, and it's a bit of a grind sometimes. It would be nice to have an assistant. You have an eye for detail, and I can teach you how to evaluate paintings, how to predict the market. But it will be hard work. Nothing like sitting in your garden and painting."

She smiled. "I'd like to try it, nevertheless."

He nodded. "All right. When can you start?"

"Monday," she said. Her mother had never really needed her. A job had been created for her, but they both knew she was redundant.

"Won't Polly mind?" he asked.

She shook her head. "On the contrary, I imagine she'll be delighted."

Polly was delighted and surprised. "I didn't think you'd want to leave the office," she admitted.

"Because Evan spends a lot of time there," Anna murmured dryly. "That's the very reason I want to leave. If I'm going to let go, I need to do it wholeheartedly. I'm very fond of Mr. Taylor, and I do like the idea of a career."

"I'd hoped you might think of marriage as one," Polly said quietly. "God knows, I'd have done that if your father had been able to settle down with me. He was too much a wanderer, though. He still is."

"You've never really dated anyone else," Anna ventured.

"Neither has he," Polly said with a smile. "Maybe someday he'll get it out of his system and come home. I never stop hoping. Meanwhile, I have a career I enjoy and I'm making gobs of money."

"That's what I want to do," Anna said seriously. "I want to do something useful with my life. Marriage—maybe someday. But not yet."

"Good girl. You're young. You have plenty of time."

"Plenty," she echoed. Her eyes were sad, but she wasn't going to moon around the house. "How about going out to eat tonight?"

"Delightful," Polly agreed. "The Beef Palace?"

Evan's favorite hangout. Anna shook her head. "How about that new Chinese restaurant, for a change?"

Polly smiled her approval. "Nice. Very nice."

As they were leaving the restaurant that night, talking animatedly about Anna's upcoming new job, Evan spotted them as he drove past with Nina. Odd, Anna eating Chinese food. He was sure she didn't like it.

"That's Polly and Anna, isn't it?" Nina murmured dryly. "I expected to have to ward Anna off at the Beef Palace tonight. They say she usually tracks you there."

Evan glowered at her. "It isn't necessary to ridicule her," he said quietly.

She stared at him blankly. "Why not? Everyone else does. It's common knowledge that she's made an utter fool of herself over you. She knows it, too."

His eyes narrowed. "You haven't said anything to her?"

She crossed her elegant legs. "I simply told her that you'd had enough of her," she replied carelessly. "She knew that already."

He winced inwardly. He knew Nina, and he couldn't imagine that she'd put it that kindly to Anna. "For God's sake," he muttered.

"She won't fare much better with her doctor friend, I'm afraid," Nina added with frank nonchalance. "He's got a wandering eye, and he'll sleep with anything in skirts. Still, it's her business."

Evan didn't say another word. He didn't even want to think about Anna.

But the next week, when he went to take the prospectus back to Polly and discuss the family's decision with her, there was no one at Anna's desk.

Polly greeted him, gesturing him into a chair as she

closed the office door and slipped into her own chair behind
the desk. "What did you decide?" she asked pleasantly.

He scowled. "Where's Anna? She isn't sick or anything?"

Polly stared. He actually sounded as though he was
worried. "Why, she's got another job, Evan," she said
haltingly. "Brand Taylor hired her."

"At the art gallery?" He sat back in the chair with a
rough sigh. "She's going to take this thing to the limit, isn't
she?" he asked curtly. "For God's sake, she didn't have to
banish herself on my account!"

Polly wisely didn't say anything. She lowered her eyes
to the prospectus he'd tossed on the desk. He didn't know
the half of it. Anna was also discussing moving out. A local
boarding house had a vacancy and she thought she might
take it, she'd told Polly over the weekend.

"The job came open unexpectedly," Polly murmured.

"Did she mention talking to Nina lately?" he persisted,
leaning forward, his dark eyes steady and unblinking on
her face.

"No," she replied. "Why?"

"Apparently Nina said some harsh things to her on my
behalf," he replied heavily. "I didn't put her up to it, but
Anna won't know that."

"It's just as well, Evan," Polly said seriously. "You and
I both know that there's no future in Anna wearing out her
heart on you. She'll get over you and marry Randall. It will
be the best thing all around."

"Randall is a playboy," he said shortly.

"If Anna loves him, it won't matter," she said, refusing
to admit that it might. "If he loves her, he'll stop chasing
other women."

"Men like that don't stop, ever," he said with narrow
eyes. "And you know it."

She smiled sadly. "Randall wouldn't be my first choice, either, Evan, but it's Anna's life. I have no right to interfere."

He leaned back again and scowled, his expression preoccupied.

"What did you decide about the prospectus?" she asked again, hoping to change the subject.

"We're going to invest," he said absently. He named a figure and abandoned his fears about Anna's future temporarily to finish discussing business.

But what she'd done bothered him. When he left Polly's office, he found himself heading straight for Taylor's Gallery.

Brand had gone to Houston for a show, leaving a nervous Anna in charge. She'd done well so far, and she was enjoying her work. But it was nerve-racking to have complete charge of the gallery by herself.

She looked lovely, Evan thought, watching her through the plate-glass window front before he entered the store. She was wearing a beige silk suit with a delicately embroidered white blouse, and her hair was in a neat French plait behind her head. She wore high heels that emphasized the graceful curve of her ankles and calves, and the fit of her suit made it apparent in the nicest of ways that she had an exquisite figure.

He opened the door and walked in, setting the bell tinkling.

Anna turned, a smile on her face that abruptly vanished when she saw him.

He felt a terrible emptiness at her expression. Always before, her eyes had brightened with gladness when she looked at him. Now it was more dread than delight that was mirrored in her blue eyes.

"Can I help you, Evan?" she asked with formal courtesy.

He moved into the gallery, glancing approvingly at the huge No Smoking sign on the wall. He stuffed his big hands into the pockets of his gray slacks and stared at her through narrowed dark eyes.

"Was it necessary to leave your mother shorthanded to avoid me?" he asked with blatant sarcasm, because her new attitude hurt him.

She lifted her delicately rounded chin to stare at him. "Since I didn't do much there in the first place except wait for you to walk in, I'd hardly call her 'left shorthanded.'"

He smiled faintly. "Is that why you're here? You don't think I have any interest in art?"

She finished dusting the frame she was holding and returned it to its position against the wall. "I don't know what your interests are aside from making money, Evan," she replied. "Did you want something?"

"I wanted to make sure Nina hadn't hurt you."

She turned, her eyebrows arching. "What difference would that make?" she asked.

He drew in a slow breath. "I didn't send her to you with any messages," he said.

"It would have served me right if you had, I guess," she confessed quietly, dropping her gaze to the floor. "I've given you a hard time."

The way she spoke made him uncomfortable. He moved closer, so that he could look down on her bright head. His hands came out of his pockets and gently framed her face to lift it to his. God, she was pretty, he thought reluctantly. Eyes like a September sky. Peaches and cream complexion. Bow lips, very pink and full and moist. Helplessly, his eyes traced them with such intensity that they parted abruptly.

"Anna," he whispered gruffly.

Her eyes widened at his tone. She'd never heard him speak that way. His gaze was hot and glittery on her mouth, and his big, warm hands had contracted around her face, tilting it up to his. With awe, she watched his head bend and his mouth come within a whisper of her lips.

"Come close," he said, his voice deep and rough. He could hear her breathing change, and all his caution vanished in a fierce rush of need. His thumbs forced her chin up as years of helpless longing knocked him off balance. "Damn it, come here!"

Trembling, her legs obeyed him even against her will, so that her slender body could feel the strength and heat of him. His suit jacket was open. His cologne drifted in to her nostrils even as she felt his chest quite suddenly against the thrust of her breasts. Contact with him was violently arousing, even through all the layers of cloth.

Her fingers pushed nervously into the soft folds of his cotton shirt and touched hard muscles. Her eyes saw nothing except the wide, hard curve of his mouth as it poised just over hers, his coffee-scented breath mingling with her own.

"Do you know how to kiss, Anna?" he asked, his head spinning with this new experience of her, his reason abruptly gone in the heat of his need for her mouth.

"Y-yes," she breathed.

"Show me."

The words went into her parted lips as his mouth suddenly crushed down over hers and took possession.

She tasted him in the sudden silence of the gallery, her body tensing, her breath stilling in her throat as she felt his hard mouth on hers for the very first time and almost fainted from the shock of pleasure its warm, expert touch gave her. He was breathing roughly. The sigh of his breath brushed her cheek. Against her breasts, his heartbeat was irregular and very hard.

Her fingers curled into his chest as she moved closer.

"Anna," he moaned hungrily.

His arms slid around her and brought her breasts crushing against him. He was very strong, and the embrace was bruising. But Anna hardly noticed in the fever he was kindling along her veins.

She lifted closer, her arms sliding under his, under the jacket, to lie against his long back. He was warm, so warm, and the feel of his powerful body was narcotic. She fed on his mouth, moaning softly as its hard crush became more insistent. She pushed upward, opening her mouth for him. When she felt his tongue accept the blatant invitation, a rush of heat made her shudder in his arms.

Evan couldn't think, couldn't breathe. This was Anna, he thought dazedly. Anna, who was too young for him. He'd pushed her away, and now he was encouraging her in the most blatant way. But he couldn't fight his own hunger. His tongue thrust fiercely into her mouth, and with each intimate thrust he imagined her body under his in bed, accepting him with this same headlong passion, her femininity yielding its secrets to him as he initiated her into lovemaking.

With a harsh groan, he lifted her against him, building the kiss into a frenzy that he almost couldn't stop in time.

Ages later he let her down again, and slowly, slowly lifted his head to look down into wide, dazed blue eyes below which her red, crushed mouth still trembled from his hot possession.

She could barely stand. He held her lightly around the waist to keep her from falling, and all the time his heartbeat sounded like a bass drum in his chest.

"You kissed me," she managed unsteadily.

"You kissed me back," he returned. His jaw clenched. He let his eyes run down her body to the opened jacket to her silk suit. Ruthlessly he moved one big hand forward to pull it aside, revealing the thrust of her breast and something more—the hard, taut nipple that signaled her arousal.

"Did you need to see…that I wanted you?" she asked tearfully. "Couldn't you tell without looking?"

"Yes, I could tell." He caught her by the waist and his hands contracted while he fought to get himself back under control. "You're nineteen," he began.

"And you're thirty-four," she said, swallowing as she managed to breathe properly again. "You don't need to explain anything to me, Evan, I know how you feel. You want me, but I'm not in the running."

His eyes darkened. "Anna…"

"Nina's more your style," she said bitterly, pushing at his chest. "She's experienced and sophisticated. I'll bet she knows as much as you do!"

She was assuming that he was sleeping with Nina. He let her keep her illusions. It wouldn't do to start making confessions now. He'd just done enough damage.

"Have you had a man yet?" he asked huskily.

She lowered her eyes, but he thrust a huge fist under her chin and made her look at him. "I said," he repeated curtly, "have you had a man?"

His eyes were a little frightening. "Don't you know?" she asked in a whisper.

She was trembling. His fist opened and he drew the backs of his fingers slowly down her arched throat and onto her soft breast, lingering while she tensed and stared at him.

"You haven't," he said with certainty. His eyes fell to his knuckles. He teased around the hard nipple, watching her body shiver and then slowly, helplessly, try to lift toward him.

"I hate you," she whimpered.

His mouth eased down to brush hers open. "Say my name," he breathed.

The nearness, the teasing, were impossible to resist, even if she really had hated him, and his hand was driving her crazy. "Evan," she moaned, lifting.

His lips opened on hers even as his hand suddenly swallowed her breast, roughly caressing her in a silence that magnified her heartbeat and his harsh breathing.

Her nails bit into his shoulders, and he shivered with pleasure. His hand contracted. She moaned into his mouth, and he wrapped one long, powerful leg around her as he moved close enough to let her feel the force of his desire.

She bit him, so aroused that she hardly realized what she was doing until she felt him groan.

Shocked, she drew back, her eyes wide and startled. "I…I didn't mean to do that," she whispered brokenly. She tried to move away, but his leg was preventing her. She felt his blatant arousal and sucked her breath in again.

He had to fight to let her go, to unwrap his body from hers. His face was hard and faintly flushed, but his eyes were angry.

"What?" he asked unsteadily.

"I…I bit you."

"And clawed me," he murmured quietly. His lips twisted into an odd smile. "You'd rip my back open in bed with those nails."

She gasped, and he suddenly realized not only what he was saying, but to whom he was saying it.

He shook his head, as if to clear it, and his brows jerked together. "Anna. For God's sake…!"

"Yes, Anna," she whispered brokenly, backing away from him. She was disheveled and wide-eyed, and shocked that she could have allowed him such liberties after the way he'd treated her. Not only allowed them, but encouraged and returned them. And in the shop, where anyone could see them! It was fortunate that the shop fronted a side street that wasn't much traveled at this time of day. It was even more fortunate that a huge painting of a Texas landscape was positioned between them and the window front. "Is Nina starving you, or is this some kind of revenge?" she asked.

He could hardly breathe. She'd been with him all the way, as passionate and fiery as he could have dreamed a woman would be. Whatever he'd kindled in her hadn't been fear. But she was nineteen, and it should never have happened.

"What do you think, honey?" he asked with faint insolence.

"I think you should go," she said quietly.

He pulled his Stetson down over his eyes. "So do I. Good luck with your new job. I'll give Nina your regards."

She didn't answer. He was out of sight and gone before she could stop trembling. If he wanted her out of his life, this was hardly the way to go about it, she thought blankly. She touched her mouth and tasted him there, shivering again with the ardor he'd aroused. Imagine being kissed like that in broad daylight, and by Evan, who didn't want her. She remembered the feel of his big body against her and flushed. Well, so much for that myth.

She went to the back of the shop long enough to fix her makeup and brush her hair, wondering if she'd ever get over what he'd done. Trying to get over him had been difficult without knowing how it felt to be held and kissed by him. From now on, it would be impossible. His body might want her, but it was patently obvious that his mind didn't. He'd probably just come to say goodbye, she kept telling herself. But why, she wondered for days afterward, had he kissed her?

## Chapter 4

All the way back to the ranch Evan's head was spinning. He'd never felt anything like that in his life, and it had to be with Anna, of all people! He groaned inwardly at the fever of passion he'd kindled in her so effortlessly; at her sweet, headlong response. In bed she would satisfy him so fully that he'd never be able to touch another woman as long as he lived. And that knowledge drove him crazy.

He had to remember the reasons he couldn't—didn't dare—let himself become involved with her. She was nineteen and a virgin. He knew instinctively that until today she'd never let a man touch her as he had. If she was really as besotted with him as everyone said she was, she'd probably been saving it all up for him, waiting for him to kiss her, to touch her. He hit the steering wheel with fierce anger at the trick fate had played on him. It was impossible! He was fifteen years her senior and a man to whom innocence was a kind of nightmare. He wanted her until she obsessed him, but he couldn't have her. He could never have her.

Innocence frightened him. Louisa's face had haunted him for years, white and rigid as he'd turned toward her after shedding his clothes. He'd thought she loved him, but she'd fought him like a tigress, screaming in terror that he was too big, too strong, he was hurting her…

He went into the house with his face like a thundercloud, his eyes blazing at the memory. Louisa had been small and thin, a fragile girl-woman whom Harden had always sworn had only tolerated his ardor because he was rich. He hadn't believed it. Louisa had loved him, as he'd loved her. Her rejection had damaged him. Although he still had the infrequent lover, now his women were sophisticated and experienced. He'd never dated an innocent since Louisa.

Harden had reminded him that Anna was a big girl, and he had to admit that she was certainly equal to his ardor. He hadn't hurt her today, and for a few seconds his strength had been unleashed when he'd forced her body into the curve of his. He couldn't believe he'd done that, gone against all his resolutions and even been oblivious enough to show her graphically how much he wanted her. He laughed bitterly, remembering the shocked look on her face, in her eyes, when he'd let her go. She'd probably never felt a man's aroused body in her life. Well, now she knew, he thought. He couldn't really imagine her lukewarm Randall ever doing anything as bold as that. He wondered absently if Randall was even aroused by Anna, because he seemed oddly passive around her, hardly noticing her. Anna must surely know that all Randall was interested in was her mother's money, but it didn't seem to matter, because she kept seeing the man.

It was none of his business, he reminded himself. From now on he had to keep out of Anna's way. He'd made a terrible error in judgment today, letting her see that he found her physically attractive. He'd have to find a way to make her believe it was a fluke, or he'd have her chasing him all over again. He couldn't afford that. The temptation to let her catch him was much too alluring.

There was a conference in Denver on a new crossbreeding program, and he packed a bag and left his brothers Donald and Harden in charge. The change of scenery might do him good. He might even meet some classy lady in Denver who could take his mind off Anna.

He didn't know it, but Anna had already decided that he was getting even with her for ignoring him, playing on her weakness for him. She flushed, remembering how quickly his body had responded to hers. It should have shocked her, but she remembered only the delight of knowing she affected him. Could he have faked that? She knew men could get aroused by thinking about women they desired. What if he'd had the delectable Nina on his mind and had used Anna to assuage his hunger for her?

She was so confused that she didn't know how to react. She didn't delude herself for a minute with thoughts that her avoidance of him had triggered those ardent kisses. He'd been so…so hateful, mocking her reactions! Almost as if he was punishing himself and her for his unexpected behavior. If only she knew what had motivated him. If only it had been because he missed her, because he cared. She could have cried at her own stupidity. He hadn't even treated her as if he respected her. Touching her that way, holding her close enough to be shocked by the vivid response of his body. Surely a man who cared about a woman wouldn't treat her like…that!

"You're very quiet lately," Polly remarked several evenings later when they were sharing a quiet supper. "Want to talk about it?"

"There's nothing, really," Anna said, forcing a smile. "I've been working very hard. Mr. Taylor said that if I'd like to do a couple of landscapes, he'll even put them in the shop. He thinks I have a talent worth developing."

"I've always thought that myself," Polly said encouragingly. She grimaced. "Although Randall didn't seem too enthusiastic about your sunflowers. He barely even looked at them, and after all the trouble I went to, having them properly matted and framed."

"Randall isn't an art lover," Anna said, defending him wanly. "He isn't musical, either."

"And you do love your classics, don't you, darling?" Polly sighed, frowning. "Anna, I don't like to interfere, but you're seeing a lot of Randall lately. Two dates this week. It isn't because of Evan, is it?"

Anna started, her face coloring. "What do you mean?"

Polly's eyes narrowed shrewdly on her daughter's face. "Evan must have hurt you very badly at that party. But don't let hurt pride send you running to the first man who shows an interest, will you? Randall's a fine man, but he has an eye to the main chance and he's something of a playboy."

"He might be, but he's not in Evan's league," Anna said bitterly.

"Evan at least sticks to women who know the score," came the dry reply. "He doesn't involve himself with innocents."

Anna kept her eyes down. It wouldn't do to tell her mother just how involved he'd been with her that day in the art gallery. "Evan is past history. I'm not running after him in dogged pursuit anymore, and he seems to find that a relief. I haven't seen him in…ages."

"He's been in Denver," Polly mentioned carelessly. "Some conference or other. Donald was supposed to go,

Harden told me, but Evan packed a bag last Thursday and took off before he could argue. A very sudden trip."

Anna had to fight not to give herself away. Last Thursday had been the day he'd kissed her so hungrily. Had he been obliged to run for fear that she might come hurrying after him for more? She flushed. Well, he needn't worry, she wasn't about to hassle him.

"Are you listening, darling?" Polly asked.

Anna lifted a serene face, smiling. "Of course."

"You worry me lately. You really do."

"No need. I'm just enjoying my new job, and growing up."

"You've done that, with a vengeance," Polly had to admit, noticing the elegant hairdo, the sleek silk pantsuit of a blue that matched Anna's eyes. "You've changed before my very eyes."

"I'm almost twenty," she reminded Polly.

"Yes. You make me feel old. I sent your father a photo of you just last month, to show him how elegant you look." The smile faded and she touched her water glass absently. "He's based in Atlanta now. He said they might move him back to Houston. If they do, he'll come and see you."

"He doesn't date," Anna mused. "You don't, either. But neither one of you will give an inch. Don't you miss him?"

"More than you know." Polly got up, all business. "But life goes on, my darling. I have to go over some figures in the study."

Anna watched her go with sad eyes. Polly had never gotten over her husband and never would. There was the hope that they might someday reconcile, but Anna knew it was a long shot. Meanwhile, she felt her mother's pain keenly.

She left the gallery after work the next day feeling

oddly restless. Randall was supposed to take her out that evening, but he'd called to cancel their date with some vague mention of night duty. It didn't matter; she wasn't in love with him, but lately he seemed to make a habit of canceling dates at the last minute, and she wondered if he was really working that much.

Her car wouldn't start, for the first time in memory. She got out and glared at it, angrily kicking a tire. It was cloudy and drizzling rain, and now she'd have to walk all the way back to the gallery to use the phone.

The roar of a truck caught her attention, and she turned just in time to see Evan pull up beside her in one of the ranch pickups with the Tremayne company's emblem on the side in bold red lettering.

"Got problems?" he asked tersely, slamming his black Stetson over one eye as he joined her. He was in working gear, chambray shirt, tight jeans, black boots and leather batwing chaps. His spurs made a faint jingling sound as he paused beside her.

"No," she lied, avoiding his eyes. "I just forgot something in the office."

His dark eyes narrowed. He knew she was lying, he could see it in the way she hesitated. Incredible that she was actually trying to avoid him.

"Your car won't start," he said flatly. "No use lying about it. I was passing when you got out and kicked it."

Her face flamed. She wouldn't meet his eyes. "I'm going to call the garage. They'll get it started."

"I'll run you over there. Get in."

"I don't want—!"

He caught her arm roughly and drew her against him, so close that she could feel the powerful threat of his body as he looked down into her shocked eyes.

"You want me," he said harshly. "I know it and so do

you. Avoiding me doesn't change that. I can feel it the minute I touch you."

Her lower lip trembled "Can't you just leave me alone?" she asked brokenly. "I know you don't want me! Do you have to make a point of it every time you see me?"

Her pain made him feel guilty. He didn't understand his own actions. The last thing he wanted to do was to hurt or humiliate her. But Denver hadn't rid him of his need for her. He hadn't been able to touch the woman who'd clung to him there. He'd intended to. He'd taken her back to his room, fed her drinks, flattered her. But when he'd pulled her into his arms and started kissing her, nothing happened. His body, for the first time, had failed him. He'd sent the woman away and cursed Anna until his voice had gone hoarse. All he could think about was the taste of her mouth. It had enraged him so much that he could hardly function for the rest of the conference, and he'd come home still fuming. His unfortunate passion for Anna was cramping his style in an unbelievable way.

His dark eyes fell to her mouth and lingered there, his fingers gripping her arm so tightly that they left bruises. "You'd give me anything I wanted," he said huskily. "Do you think I don't know how vulnerable you are?"

She shivered. This wasn't the Evan she knew. This man was a stranger, sensual, domineering, frightening. "This isn't fair, Evan," she choked.

"Is what you do to me fair?" he asked coldly.

"I…haven't done anything to you, except avoid you," she said miserably. "I thought that was what you wanted."

His other hand moved to her waist and drew her slowly against the powerful length of him, against lean muscle that rippled where she touched it. She gasped as her hand caught at his shirt, her eyes going involuntarily to the thick pelt of hair that showed in the opening at the collar.

"This is what I want," he said, his voice deep and quiet as his hand slid to the base of her spine and moved her hips gently against his. He caught his breath audibly as the feel of her kindled the kind of arousal he hadn't felt since his sixteenth birthday. He laughed bitterly at the irony of it, because he couldn't seem to feel that with another woman, having had a taste of Anna.

"It isn't funny," she moaned, pushing at his chest with her face gone scarlet. "Evan, stop!"

His hand withdrew, but he still had her by the arm. "Funny, isn't it?" he asked, his eyes glittering. "The joke of the century, that a virgin should have that effect on me when an experienced woman can't even…" He bit off the words, suddenly pushing Anna away. He was breathing roughly, and his arousal was so obvious that Anna averted her eyes in something like panic. He saw her embarrassment, and it angered him.

"I have to go," she said unsteadily.

"Still seeing the beloved physician?" he asked.

She wouldn't look at him. "If you mean Randall, yes."

"Why don't you marry him? It would get you out of my hair, at least."

Tears stung her eyes. "I've been out of your hair for weeks, haven't you noticed?" she asked, glaring up at him. His eyes were shadowed, but she thought she saw the flicker of his eyelashes. "I haven't come near you! It's you who are harassing me!"

"Turn about," he said softly, his eyes glittery. "How do you like it?"

"I hate it!" she raged.

"So did I, baby," he replied coldly. "Every minute, every day that you hounded me. Thank God for Nina, she must have finally convinced you that it was never going to work.

Even a man who cares about a woman can't stomach that kind of harrassment."

Her eyes closed, containing the tears. "You've made your point," she said in a haunted tone. "May I go now?"

He felt sick all over when he looked at her face. He shouldn't be this cruel to her. It wasn't her fault that he wanted her to the exclusion of other women. She was just a child, despite her lovely curves, just a little girl. And he was savaging her. He came to his senses in a painful jerk.

"Anna…"

Her eyes opened, blue as the sky, wet with tears and pain. "I'm sorry!"

His teeth ground together in a grimace of anguish. He moved toward her, but she turned and started to run across the street, back toward the gallery.

Evan watched her until she was out of sight, his face drawn with guilt and remorse. He felt as if he'd just torn the wings from a butterfly.

Anna was pale and unnaturally quiet when she got home, having found a mechanic to fix her car. But Polly was out, to Anna's relief, and Anna managed to get to bed without being seen. Now that she knew what Evan really thought of her, she didn't know how she was going to stay alive. He seemed to actually hate her.

The next few weeks dragged by, with Evan taunting her at every corner. He brought Nina in to buy paintings at the gallery, making his attentiveness to her so evident that Anna wanted to scream. He was seen around town with her, and seemed to go out of his way to make sure that Anna saw them. As revenge went, it was pure mastery. Anna felt as if she'd been cut to pieces, even if she did manage to salvage a little pride by stepping up her dates with Randall.

A month after Evan had made his last cruel taunt, she

went to a concert with Randall and found Evan and Nina sitting only three seats away from them. It hurt to see the two of them together, with Evan so loving and attentive to Nina that the other woman seemed actually to purr when he touched her.

During the intermission, Randall went to get punch for himself and Anna, and Nina went to the powder room. It was almost fate, Anna thought miserably, that threw her directly in Evan's path while their respective dates were missing.

"Enjoying yourself, honey?" Evan asked her with a smile that didn't begin to reach his eyes. "Or is the beloved physician just a poor substitute for me?"

She shivered, glaring at him. "Randall is good company."

"Is he?" he mused. "He seems to pay more attention to the music than he does to you. Or is that what you like?"

"It beats having him all over me," she blurted out, and then blushed furiously at Evan's soft, mocking laughter.

"Nina likes being touched," he said, his eyes holding hers. "She opens her mouth when I kiss her, and melts under my body…."

"Damn you," Anna choked, tears burning her eyes. "I've never hated anyone in my life as much as I hate you!"

It would have hurt less if she'd slapped him. His face hardened. "It beats having you run after me begging to be made love to," he returned hotly.

She whirled, shaking all over, and made her way to Randall. She held on to his sleeve as if she was afraid she'd drown if she turned it loose. Behind her a tall man with dark eyes flinched at his own merciless behavior, wondering how he could have allowed it to go this far. His hunger for Anna grew daily, until it was an ache that almost brought him to his knees. He'd been fighting a losing battle for weeks, and tonight, he lost it. Being cruel to her was the only protection he had left, but that was no longer bearable. He sighed wearily, his eyes lovingly tracing the long lines of her body, adoring her silently. She was so lovely. All his sweetest dreams rolled together.

It was no good, he admitted finally. He was only fooling himself that he could fight her hold on him. He smiled ruefully. Tomorrow, he'd go by the gallery and take her to lunch and admit defeat. He hoped she wouldn't be too unforgiving. He turned back to find Nina approaching him, his mouth set in a hard, uncompromising line.

Anna was silent for the rest of the concert. She didn't look toward Evan again, refusing to glance at him even though he seemed to spend the better part of the evening trying to force her to look his way. She clung to Randall and rushed him outside when the concert ended, desperate not to have to see Evan and Nina together again.

She and Randall walked home, because the civic center was just two blocks away from Anna's house.

"I'll go into private practice next year," Randall was telling her, his eyes dreamy. "I want to set up in Houston. There's an older, established doctor in one of the ritzier parts of town. I've already inquired about buying into his practice." He glanced down at her. "If we got married, say around December, we could move in by late January."

She stopped walking and looked up at him. "You mean, you could buy into the practice if my mother gave us a substantial cash wedding present," she said matter-of-factly. What he was hinting at was suddenly welcome. She wanted so desperately to get out of Evan's reach forever, to avoid any more heartbreaking torment from him.

He was taken aback at the calm way she said it. "Anna…"

"I know you're not dying of love for me, Randall," she

said quietly. "I know that there have been other women. It doesn't matter. I might as well marry you as anybody else. Why not?"

He felt guilty for the first time as he saw the dead look in her eyes. He didn't love her, but he was fond of her. He frowned. "You make it sound like a business proposition."

"It is. My mother would stake us. You're ambitious, so you'll work hard and make a name for yourself. I can entertain. I'll find things to keep me busy. Maybe I'll paint." She put away her dreams of Evan and a houseful of children for the last time. She had to be practical.

"You'll marry me?" he asked.

She nodded.

He sighed, and drew her into his arms, holding her lightly. "You deserve something better than this," he said unexpectedly.

She laid her cheek against his chest and smiled. "Sometimes, Randall, you're a very nice man."

"Not often. I'm all too aware of my limitations. I like women, and for some reason they like me, even if I'm not handsome." He smoothed her long hair. "I like being with you, because I can be myself. I'll take care of you, Anna. I'll try to be discreet…"

"It won't matter." And it wouldn't. He couldn't touch her heart, so she was safe. "We'll tell Mama when we get home."

He nodded. He took her hand and smiled down at her as they walked back toward the house. Anna smiled back, but nothing helped the ache inside her.

"You're getting married?" Polly stammered when they told her the news, automatically registering that neither of them seemed particularly ecstatic or overjoyed at the prospect.

"That's right," Randall said pleasantly. "I hope you'll wish us well, Mrs. Cochran. I'll take care of Anna."

It would have made Polly a little happier if he'd said he loved Anna. She glanced at her daughter and wanted to weep at the composed features, the dull eyes. Anna was only doing this because of Evan; she knew it. But her daughter was old enough to make her own decisions, however wrong they might be.

"Of course I'll congratulate you," Polly said, forcing a smile. "I hope you'll be very happy. Now when are you planning to be married?"

"At Christmas," Anna said quietly.

Randall nodded. "I can take a couple of days off and we'll have a brief honeymoon."

"Randall wants to buy into a practice in Houston," Anna added, thinking that Houston would be a good place to live, because she wouldn't ever have to see Evan again.

"I'll help with that, of course," Polly said brusquely, and watched relief shadow Randall's eyes. Damn him! She didn't want to buy her daughter a husband, but what could she say? Anna was living on her nerves already. Evan was obviously not interested in her, either. He was being seen everywhere with Nina, flaunting his relationship. He'd even brought the woman to Polly's office with him, making his interest in her so evident that half the staff must have mentioned it to Anna. She wondered if that had been his intention. He seemed to go out of his way lately to taunt Anna, right down to parading Nina past the art gallery at lunch every day.

Polly had never thought of Evan as a particularly cruel man, but Anna seemed to trigger it in him. Odd, when Anna was the type of woman who particularly needed kindness. She certainly wouldn't find any in Evan. Polly pursed her lips. This engagement might not be a bad idea, after all. Once he knew Anna was marrying, he might relent and stop hurting her.

"We'll have to go shopping for an engagement ring tomorrow," Randall told Anna, smiling. "What would you like?"

She smiled back. He was a good friend, even if she couldn't work up a grand passion for him. "I'd like an emerald solitaire," she said.

Randall's eyebrows arched. "Emerald?"

"I don't like traditional stones," she said gently. "And a small emerald and diamond wedding band. Later, when you're wildly successful, you can buy me something big and flashy, okay?"

He grimaced. She made him feel mean and guilty. "Anna, I'd buy you a trunkful of diamonds if I had the money," he said, and suddenly meant it. "God knows, you're worth them."

Polly raised her eyebrows and smiled. That sounded more promising. Randall might turn out to be a worthy son-in-law after all. If only Anna loved him.

"We could go from the gallery to pick it up," Anna suggested, "about noon."

Noon. That was when Evan usually escorted Nina past her window. Polly turned, smothering a grin. Good for Anna. It wouldn't hurt to let Evan know that she wasn't pining away for love of him anymore.

"It's a date," Randall said, smiling. "Now, you'd better walk me to the door. I've got exams the rest of the week, so except for getting the ring, we won't see too much of each other."

"That's okay," Anna said demurely. "We'll make up for it when we're together. There's a new exhibit at the zoo, tropical amphibians."

"Fantastic!" Randall enjoyed the study of herpetology as a hobby, and Anna shared his fascination with exotic frogs and lizards. It had been surprising, and pleasing, to find that they had a few things in common. He hated art and music, although he humored Anna by attending concerts. But he really enjoyed going to the zoo, and so did she. It was something to build on, at least.

Anna was thinking the same thing. She wouldn't have an ecstatic marriage, but she'd settle for a little harmony. God knew, she could never have had that with Evan. For a kind, pleasant man, he seemed to grow fangs when he came within a few feet of her. She affected him in a very negative way, so it was probably just as well that she was marrying Randall. But inside, her dreams died.

## Chapter 5

Anna thought she'd never get through the next morning. Only the thought that Randall was coming for her made it bearable. If she had to watch Evan with Nina, it would be for the last time. Presumably when he heard about her engagement, he'd realize that she'd given up on him and maybe then he'd leave her alone and stop taunting her with what she couldn't have. The humiliation of knowing that Evan was totally aware of her helpless passion for him was unbearable. Having him flaunt Nina at her was worse.

Sure enough, at ten minutes before noon, Evan came past the window as he did now every day. But he was alone this time. Nina wasn't with him.

Anna clenched her hands together in front of her, grateful that Mr. Taylor was in the gallery, going over their frame inventory, when Evan walked in the door. At least she wasn't on her own.

"Well, hello, Evan," Brand Taylor said with a smile. "Nice to see you. Anything in particular you're looking for?"

Evan was taken aback. He hadn't planned on Taylor being in. Most days, when he went past the gallery Anna was alone. Today, of all days, she wasn't.

"No, I'm…browsing, thanks," Evan said.

"Go ahead, then. Anna can help you with prices, if you see something you like."

Anna wasn't looking at him, though. Her eyes were almost frantic, riveted to the front door. His face hardened. Was she hoping to be rescued? Remembering his recent treatment of her, he realized that he couldn't blame her. He'd tried so hard to resist his hunger for her, but he couldn't quite live without her. He'd cope somehow with his fears, he'd have to. But her face wasn't encouraging, and he had a flash of panic as he realized that he might already be too late. She looked…

He hesitated, his dark eyes sweeping over her. She'd lost weight. The beige suit she wore didn't fit as closely as it had, and there were new lines in that pretty face, new hollows under her high cheekbones. She looked elegant and brittle.

He moved toward her, hating the way she jerked around and took a step backward when she saw him coming. Had he hurt her so badly?

Her eyes glanced off his gray suit and pearly Stetson. He was dressed for travel, she imagined, not knowing that he'd worn his best clothes just to see her.

"Was there something you wanted to know?" she asked in a forcibly steady tone, and made herself look at him.

Her eyes were deep blue and full of pain. It hurt him to see it and know that it was because of him.

"Yes," he said, his voice almost hesitant. His eyes fell to her soft mouth and back up to hold her gaze. "Anna, I…"

The bell on the front door drew their attention. Randall came in, smiling at Mr. Taylor before he walked to Anna's side. He knew how she felt about Evan Tremayne, and protective instincts he didn't even know he had welled up inside him. He slid an arm around her waist and kissed her forehead with deliberate possession, not missing the flash of Evan's stormy eyes or the surprise on his dark face.

"Hello, darling," he told Anna gently. "Ready to go?"

"Yes," Anna choked. "I'll just get my purse."

"We're picking out the rings today," Randall told Evan levelly. "Anna and I are getting married at Christmas."

Getting married. Getting married. Getting married. Evan heard the words echo in his mind until he thought he'd gone mad. Anna was going to marry Randall. They were going to pick out rings. He'd come here today to apologize to her, on his knees if necessary, to ask her out on what would have been their first real date. He was going to try to build a relationship with her. But Randall had beat him to it. He'd hurt her, tormented her into accepting Randall's proposal. For the rest of his life, he'd have to live with that. She didn't love Randall or want him, but she was going to marry him.

"You might congratulate us," Randall prompted. "I'm going to make her happy. I swear I am."

How can you, Evan was wondering bitterly, when she loves me? But he didn't say it. He rammed his hands into his pockets, drawing the fine fabric of his slacks taut over powerfully muscled legs, and his eyes smoldered as they went to Anna's pale face.

"I'm ready when you are, Randall," Anna told him quietly, and Evan had to look hard even to recognize that she was the same woman he'd known only weeks ago. The bright spark, the impish nature might never have been. Anna had matured to middle-age overnight, gone calm and quiet and elegant. At that moment he'd have given anything to see her the way she was.

"I'm coming. See you around, Evan," he told the older man, smiling as he went to take Anna's arm.

Evan watched them go with dead eyes. She was going to marry Randall. And when she looked up and met his gaze, he knew why. She was doing it to show him that she wasn't chasing him anymore, that he was free of her, because that was what she thought he wanted. Heaven knew, he'd given her more than enough reason to think so.

"Oh, God, no!" he ground out in a tortured whisper and started toward them. He had to stop her.

But as he nodded to Taylor and left the shop, Nina drove up to the curb and called to him.

"There you are!" she waved gaily. "I missed you at the office, so I thought I'd meet you here!"

Anna heard her, but she didn't look back. What a good thing Randall had come for her. She'd thought, hoped, that Evan might have come just to see her, but he'd been meeting Nina there, flaunting her again. No wonder he'd been in such a rush to get out of the gallery, and she'd dared to dream he was coming after her! Well, so much for dead hopes.

She slid her hand into Randall's and walked along beside him, half-numb, listening while he told her what he'd planned for the weekend. He might as well have been giving her a weather report, for all the interest she showed.

That afternoon, after work, she went home alone. On an impulse, she stopped by the civic center to see what concerts were planned for the weekend. Randall's emerald solitaire winked in the soft light, gracing her long, slender hand. The symbol of his intention to marry her, and it didn't even touch her heart. She was saving Evan from herself, she thought bitterly, that was all. She didn't dare think about what marriage to Randall would be like, or she'd go mad.

Tears stung her eyes and began to roll down her cheeks while she stood there. And she suddenly realized, horrified, that Miranda Tremayne was standing beside her.

"Oh, Anna," the older woman said, grimacing. She put her arms around Anna without even thinking, comforting her.

It was so unexpected that Anna was totally without a defense. She cried until her throat hurt, grateful that pedestrian traffic was almost nonexistent for the moment. She pulled away finally, and Miranda produced a tissue out of the pocket of her maternity dress.

"Feel better?" she asked gently. "It's Evan, isn't it?" she added with resignation, nodding at Anna's surprised look. "Yes, I know. We all know what he's been doing, throwing Nina in your face. I used to think that Evan was a big teddy bear, but Harden wasn't kidding when he told me Evan had fangs. I never dreamed he could be so cruel."

"I drove him to it," Anna sniffed. "It's my own fault."

"He could have stopped it anytime he wanted to, just by having a quiet word with you," Miranda said angrily. "This isn't like him. He's been terrible at home ever since he came back from Denver."

"He hates me," Anna said unsteadily. "I'm not kidding. I mean, he really hates me! He made fun of the way I felt about him and laughed at Randall...I'm marrying Randall," she added weakly, showing her ring. "Isn't it pretty? We're going to live in Houston." She burst into tears again. "Oh, I am sorry," she apologized, red eyed. "I didn't realize how much he hated me. It must have embarrassed him terribly when I ran after him!"

Miranda could have backed a truck over Evan with

pure delight at the moment. She patted Anna's shoulder awkwardly. "That doesn't mean he has any right to hurt you like this."

"This is just the aftershock," Anna said stubbornly, dabbing at her eyes. "Once Randall and I are married, I'll be fine."

"Not if you love Evan," Miranda said sadly.

Anna ground her teeth together, but her lower lip trembled ominously. "I'll stop loving him," she choked. "I'll have to."

"Evan keeps secrets," Miranda said slowly. "I don't know what they are and Harden won't tell me. But there's some reason for the way he treats you."

"It's my age," Anna replied. "He thinks I'm a child."

"There's more to it than that, I'm sure of it," Miranda replied. "Anna, I wish there was something I could do."

Anna smiled at her. "You're very kind," she said. "Harden's so lucky, to have someone like you. He was worse than Evan, you know. Most women around here were scared to death of him. He could look right through you."

"He's mellowed." Miranda grinned, patting her stomach. "Not that he's tame. None of the Tremayne men are. But he's all I'll ever want."

"I think that would go double for him," Anna said softly and smiled. "I have to go. You won't…mention that I was standing out here bawling my head off?"

"I won't tell Evan anything, Anna," came the gentle reply. "But I do wish you'd reconsider what you're doing."

"I'm doing the only thing I can, short of joining the French Foreign Legion." Anna sighed. "I'll be happy with Randall."

Miranda wanted to question that cool statement, but she couldn't. Anna was headstrong and stubborn, and she seemed perfectly capable of cutting off her nose to spite her face. As for Evan...

She went home fuming. Harden was sitting in the living room with his mother, Theodora, when Miranda walked in and flung her purse on a chair.

"Are you all right?" Harden asked, immediately concerned.

"Oh, you mean the checkup," she said, preoccupied. "Yes, I'm fine. The doctor says I'm progressing beautifully." She bent to kiss him gently. She smiled down at him, her love echoing back from his glittery blue eyes. "The baby is just fine."

"Thank God." He sighed. "The way you looked when you came in spooked me."

"I want to kill your brother," she told him.

"Which one?" he returned.

Theodora chuckled as she worked her embroidery thread into a complicated floral design. "Evan," she guessed.

"How did you know?" he queried.

"He's the only bachelor left."

"Good point," Miranda agreed, "and I hope he gets to stay that way for life. If you could have seen Anna..."

"What about Anna?" Harden asked softly.

"He's cut her to pieces. She was in tears. And that's not the worst of it. She's going to marry Randall."

Harden's face went taut. "She doesn't love him."

"It's to show Evan that she's through chasing him, I know it is," Miranda said miserably. "She's running, and you know as well as I do that he's given her every reason in the world to want to get away from him. She's convinced that he hates her."

"He acts like it lately," Harden had to admit.

Theodora looked up from her needlework. "Love and

hate are twins, you know. You can't hate somebody unless you can love them."

"He's never been in love, not really," Harden replied. "Oh, he thought he was. He had a bad experience, and it's blinded him to a lot of things. Anna's not his problem. It's all in his mind."

"What are you talking about?" Miranda chided.

"I can't tell you without breaking a confidence," he said. He smiled at her. "No secrets, I know, but this is Evan's, not mine. You'll have to let him deal with it."

"He's waited too late," Theodora said sadly. "I'm sorry. Anna's very young, but she's sweet and generous and loving. He could do so much worse."

"I hope Randall will be kind to her." Miranda sighed. "But I'm not sorry for Evan," she added angrily. "He didn't deserve her in the first place. I hope he marries that Nina of his, and I hope she gives him hell twice a day!"

Theodora laughed at her rage, but Harden didn't. He knew what Evan was afraid of, why he was running from Anna. What a pity that he couldn't face the threat of his own strength and deal with it. Now he'd lost the one woman in the world who'd ever really loved him. Harden felt sorry for him.

For days after that, Evan kept to himself, not even talking to the people around him. He threw himself into ranch work with a zest that surprised and exhausted his own men, because while he was punishing himself, they had to suffer with him. He pushed them during the late summer roundup of bulls until one of them quit, which was what finally brought him to his senses.

"I've never seen so many cowboys in church on Sunday," Theodora mused when they had supper that night. "They all seem to say the same thing—please, God, save us from Evan."

"Cut it out," Evan muttered. He didn't smile. He hadn't

for a long time. The lighthearted man Miranda remembered from her first days at the ranch might never have been.

"God, you remind me of myself," Harden remarked dryly, glancing down the table at him. "All bristles and thorns lately."

Evan didn't answer him. He finished his coffee and got up. "I'll see you later."

"Taking Nina out again?"

"Who else?" Evan replied without looking at him. He kept walking.

Miranda just shook her head. He got worse by the day.

Evan had taken Nina to a play in Houston, but he was surprised and infuriated to find Randall there—with a woman who was definitely not Anna. This one was tall and brunette and wearing a dress that left nothing at all to the imagination.

He cornered the man at intermission, his dark eyes threatening.

"I thought you were engaged," he said curtly.

"I am," Randall replied. "This is my cousin Nell."

Evan glanced at the woman and laughed shortly. "Sure she is."

"Listen," Randall said curtly, "Anna and I have an arrangement which is none of your business."

"Does she know you're out with Cousin Nell?" Evan persisted.

"No, but she will, because I never had any intention of covering it up," Randall replied honestly. "At least Anna will be better off with me than she would with you," he added coldly. "I'll never cut her up the way you did."

Evan exploded. He actually reached toward the other man, but a crowd of returning patrons interrupted the movement and he regained his control. He turned on his heel, rejoining Nina.

"What was that all about?" Nina demanded petulantly. "Trying to live Anna's life for her again?"

He looked down at her with eyes that threatened. She actually backed away.

"Anna is my business, not yours," he said, every word measured and dangerous.

Nina swallowed. "Don't you mean, she's Randall's? After all, it's him she's engaged to."

He took her arm and escorted her back to their seats. He didn't say another word to her then or later.

The next day he stopped by Polly's office on the pretense of business. But once the door was closed and he was sitting comfortably in one of her wing chairs, he tossed his hat aside and leaned forward intently.

"Randall was out on the town in Houston last night with some brunette," he said shortly. "He's already two-timing Anna, and they aren't even married yet."

Polly was shocked, not only by the information, but by the anger in Evan's voice as he told her about it.

"What kind of marriage is it going to be, for God's sake?" he ground out. "Her pride won't stand that kind of treatment!"

"Evan, I appreciate your concern," Polly said quietly. "But it's Anna's life."

"My God, she's ruining it!" he exclaimed, throwing up his hands. "Don't you care?"

Polly's eyebrows lifted. "Aren't you the man who's been doing his best to chase her into Randall's arms for the past few months?"

He grimaced. "I thought it would be the best thing for her," he said shortly. "Randall's going to make a good doctor, a good provider. I figured once they got engaged, he'd at least be discreet about his affairs."

"He is," Polly replied. "Houston is a long way from Jacobsville."

"If I saw him, other people from here could."

Polly leaned back in her chair, studying his angry face. "Evan, how do you know the woman he was with wasn't his cousin?"

He let out a rough sigh and rested his forehead on his bunched hands. "My God, I don't. But you know what he's like."

"Yes. And so does Anna. She'll be amply provided for, and she'll keep busy in Houston. That's where they're going to live when they're married."

It was killing him. Killing him! He got to his feet with a harsh groan, grabbing up his Stetson.

"Anna thinks you hate her," she said, noticing that he didn't face her, that his back was rigid. "Do her a favor and let her keep on thinking it."

He twisted the Stetson in his hands. "Why shouldn't I?" he asked huskily. "It's the truth."

"Is it, really, Evan?" she asked softly.

He didn't answer her. He slammed the Stetson over one eye and went out, without ever looking back.

Polly watched him leave and felt a twinge of sorrow for all of them. Evan loved Anna. If she'd ever wondered about his feelings, she knew now. It was a raging, helpless kind of love that he was fighting with everything in him, tearing her to pieces to keep her from seeing how vulnerable he really was. And Anna loved him, deathlessly. But neither of them was going to give in, least of all Evan, who for reasons of his own wanted no part of loving. Polly could have wept. She wished she could tell her daughter, but it would serve no purpose. Evan wasn't going to give in to it, she knew that instinctively, but if Anna went too close to him, he'd savage her. He might have already done that.

Polly knew he'd been taunting her. She was sure he hated her. It was just as well. She could do worse than Randall, and perhaps someday, she'd even get over Evan.

Sure, she thought bitterly, as she pulled out the portrait of her husband, Duke, that she kept in her desk drawer, just like I've gotten over you. He looked a lot like Anna—blond and blue-eyed. He was tall and slender, and Polly had loved him just as passionately as Anna loved Evan. But they'd never been able to live together, because he had wanderlust. She didn't like remembering how she'd begged to go with him, or how he'd told her, so gently, that he couldn't drag her around the world with a baby in her arms. Slowly she brought the picture to her lips and kissed it before she put it away. So much for looking back. She had work to do. She pushed the intercom button and called her secretary in for dictation.

Randall told Anna about the woman he'd taken to the play, because he knew Evan would make sure she found out. As he'd expected, she didn't bat an eyelash.

"I don't see anything so terrible about it." She shrugged. "Why did you feel obliged to tell me?"

"Because Evan was there and went crazy when he saw me with another woman," he said shortly, ramming his hands in his pockets. "He very nearly threw a punch at me."

Anna's heart jumped, but she schooled her face not to betray the shock of pleasure she felt at Evan's displeasure. "He's very old-fashioned," she began.

"Like the rest of the Tremaynes, I know." He sighed. "Well, I'm never going to be Mr. Faithful, Anna," he added with a rueful smile. "I'm sorry. It's not in me."

"I know that." She changed the subject abruptly, offering him coffee. He watched her make it and was suddenly grateful that he didn't love her. If he had, seeing how indifferent she was to his amours would kill him. She was going to live and die in love with Evan Tremayne. He pitied her. He pitied Evan more. There were worse things for a man than marrying a woman who loved him passionately. Evan had thrown away a precious gift and didn't even know it.

Polly mentioned that Evan had been by the office and had talked about seeing Randall in Houston. It amazed Anna that he'd been so persistent. But she was even more surprised to find him waiting for her at the gallery when she went to open it the next morning in Mr. Taylor's absence.

"It's about time," Evan said curtly, glaring at her as she produced the key.

Her heart jumped, but she schooled her face not to show the dangerous excitement he fostered in her. She'd learned the hard way to keep a poker face these days. "What do you want?" she asked quietly.

He followed her into the gallery, formidable in tan denims and a blue-checked Western shirt, his old black Stetson slanted arrogantly over one dark eye. "You know what I want. How long are you going to let Randall drag your pride through the dirt before you do something about it? Or don't you care that he's having women on the side?"

She put her purse down and turned on the lights, very elegant in her tailored gray suit, with her hair in a neat chignon. "Randall is a grown man. I don't mind if he takes another woman to the theater when I'm not available."

"Why weren't you available?" he demanded. "You're engaged, aren't you?"

"I had a headache," she said inadequately.

"Already?" he asked with a cold mocking smile. "I thought that came after your wedding night."

She turned on him like a wounded thing. "Get out!" she cried. "Leave me alone!"

He moved closer, the slowness of his movements imparting a sensual threat. "That isn't what you want," he said, his voice deep and slow and soft.

She backed away until the counter stopped her, her eyes wide and frightened as they met his.

He eased his hands onto the counter on either side of her, gently pinning her there with the threat of his body. He smelled of spice and leather and she had to close her eyes to keep her hands away from the expanse of broad, hair-roughened chest in front of her, where the snaps had come apart at his collarbone.

"Does it bother you to look at me?" he asked quietly.

Her eyes opened, and he read the vulnerability in them, the helpless attraction. Her gaze went to his chest and was jerked back to his eyes.

"So that's it," he said, almost to himself. He moved one hand to his shirt and, holding her eyes, ripped the snaps open down the front, baring the bronze, muscular chest under its thick mat of dark, curling hair. "Touch me," he said curtly.

Her lips parted. She couldn't believe this was happening, here in the gallery, in broad daylight.

"It's all right," he said quietly. He caught her hands and put them inside his shirt, pressing them gently into the thickness of body hair.

"Evan!" she moaned.

His breath caught as he pushed her hands closer. "Oh, God," he managed as his body suddenly went taut with violent arousal. "Pull, baby," he breathed, bending to her mouth. "Get a handful of it and pull…!"

She did, arching up to the open warmth of his mouth even as it met hers. He groaned as her hands grew bolder, caressing him, tugging at the thick growth of hair, glorying in his masculinity, in his size, his strength.

He lifted her suddenly onto the counter so that he was between the folds of her full skirt, between her thighs. His mouth bent, nuzzling under the jacket to find the soft silk of her blouse and the softer warmth of her breast. His mouth opened on the hard tip, taking it inside his lips along with the fabric.

"Ev…an, no!" she cried, shuddering at the sheer ecstasy of his mouth on her body. But even as she protested, her head arched back and her hands went trembling into his thick brown hair, dislodging his hat, to hold him to her body.

"You're mine," he whispered, nibbling softly at her nipple. "You belong to me. I'm not giving you to Randall."

He lifted his head suddenly and moved back, breathing unsteadily, his eyes dark and smoldering as they met hers. He looked down at the damp fabric over her breast with pure masculine triumph. "Do you let Randall do that to you?" he asked mockingly.

She could barely breathe. The sight of him like that—his hair disheveled, his shirt open and wrinkled over his bare chest, his mouth faintly swollen from its hard pressure against her body made her dizzy. What he was saying finally registered, though, and made her flush scarlet. She'd actually let him touch her in that intimate way, given in without a fight, and he was mocking her for it. She felt a wave of shame.

"No, you don't," he answered his own question, his eyes blazing into hers. "You've never let anybody do to you what you'll let me. You never will."

She was trembling, but the bold statement wounded her pride. He was telling her that he owned her, and that wasn't true. She couldn't let him humiliate her again.

He lifted her down from the counter, kissing her with careless tenderness before he lazily resnapped the pearly buttons of his shirt. "Give Randall back the ring," he said with a satisfied smile.

She pulled the jacket over the wet spot on her blouse, red-faced. She could still feel his mouth on her there. He must think she was easy, to treat her like that, like some loose woman. "No," she said huskily.

His hands paused. "What?"

She moved away from him to the door, deliberately opening it. "You wanted to show me that I can't resist you. All right, you've done it. Now you can go and laugh about it with Nina. But I'm going to marry Randall."

"For God's sake, why?" he burst out angrily, almost crushing the Stetson in his big hand. "You don't love him!"

She lifted her eyes to his without flinching. "That *is* why," she said hoarsely. "Because I don't love him. Because he can never hurt me the way you have. Is your pride satisfied now, Evan?" she asked. "Has humiliating me healed it?"

He drew in a sharp breath. "Anna, that isn't why I came," he began.

"I'd like you to go, please."

"You don't understand," he said angrily, pausing in front of her. "I came to explain something to you."

She closed her eyes, tears threatening. "Please, can't you stop hurting me?" she whispered brokenly. "I'm getting married, I'm leaving Jacobsville because of you…isn't that enough?"

"Because of me?" he asked hesitantly, scowling.

Her face lifted, her eyes opening, tormented. "I can't help…what I feel," she sobbed. "Why must you keep punishing me for it?"

"Oh, baby, no," he said, horrified. "Anna, I didn't come here to hurt you!"

"I don't ever want to see you again, Evan," she whispered. "If your friendship with my mother and me ever meant anything to you, then, please just go away."

"And let you make the biggest mistake of your life by marrying that pill-peddling philanderer?"

"At least he never treated me like a tramp!" she all but screamed at him.

Evan stiffened. "I haven't. Not ever."

"What would you call what you just did to me?" she asked, clutching the jacket closer, horrified at her own actions, at her response.

He began to realize just how innocent she was, how untouched. He let out a slow breath. "Anna, what I did to you…that's part of lovemaking," he said gently. "It's nothing to be ashamed of."

She went scarlet. "If you don't leave, I'll scream," she threatened, her eyes wet now.

He threw up his hands. "All right. But this isn't the end of it," he said shortly.

"Yes, it is," she cried. "Go away!"

He went out the door, his mind already spinning with ways to pry her out of Randall's arms. But Anna closed the door and wept. She knew he didn't care about her now. He couldn't, and treat her like—like that! And worst of all was the memory that she'd let him. How could she ever face herself in the mirror again?

# Chapter 6

Polly noticed how upset Anna was at supper. She didn't want to pry, but she was worried about the way her daughter was losing weight and brooding.

"Can I help?" she asked Anna gently.

Anna's head jerked up and she flushed. "Uh, no, but thank you."

"Something's wrong," Polly said. "Did Randall do something to upset you?"

Anna shook her head. "It wasn't Randall."

"Evan?"

Anna flushed.

Polly smiled gently. "I should have known. He went to see you, didn't he? And had plenty to say about Randall taking that woman to the theater."

"How did you know?" Anna asked.

"He came to see me, too," Polly said, smiling ruefully. "He'd worked himself into a real lather over it. Amazing how possessive he is about you, for a man who professes not to be interested in you." Her eyes narrowed shrewdly when Anna's flush got worse. "He did more than just talk, too, didn't he?"

Anna's lower lip trembled as she lifted her coffee cup to her lips and took a sip. "He treated me like some woman he'd picked up for the night," she said huskily.

Polly's eyebrows rose. That didn't sound like Evan. "He kissed you?"

"Yes, and then he put his mouth on my...my..." She broke off, unable to put it into words.

Polly only smiled. "Darling, I've sheltered you too much, haven't I?" She touched Anna's cold hand. "Anna, nothing is, or should be, taboo in lovemaking between a man and a woman, as long as they both enjoy it," she said gently. "Because a man touches you, or kisses you, in a less than conventional way, it doesn't mean he has a low opinion of you. Where did you get such ideas?"

"Well, you never talk about it," Anna mumbled.

"You've never asked me." She studied the tormented young face. "Did you enjoy what he did, Anna?"

The younger woman's eyes closed. "Oh, yes," she whispered. "But I shouldn't have let him, and he shouldn't have touched me like that. I'm engaged!"

"To a man who doesn't even want you," Polly said quietly. "I'd rather see you have a blazing affair with Evan than marry a man you don't love, Anna."

"Mama!"

"Well, I would," Polly said stubbornly. "At least Evan wants you. I can't imagine him going out with another woman if it was him you were engaged to. Can you?"

"He's not like Randall."

"No, he isn't. He's passionate and stubborn and more man than most women could ever handle." She searched

Anna's face. "He's a very big man, Anna. There was some talk once about his having hurt a woman badly in bed."

Anna flushed, her eyes meeting Polly's. "Deliberately?" she whispered.

"Of course not. But he's uncommonly strong, and a man can't always control his passion when he's aroused. The woman he was dating was half his size, a fragile little thing and very innocent. I don't know if that has anything to do with his attitude toward you, but it's a possibility."

"I'm not small and fragile," Anna reminded her mother.

"I know. But you're very innocent. Virginity can be an impossible obstacle for some men, especially men who are already afraid of their strength. It's something to think about."

"He didn't seem very afraid of it this morning," Anna recalled.

"Kissing is one thing. Sex is quite another."

She cleared her throat. "I won't have an affair with Evan."

"I never thought you would," Polly replied calmly. "But if he's really interested in you, it wouldn't hurt to reconsider marrying Randall. Evan's twice the man he is."

"Evan hates me," she said unsteadily. "He looks at me as if he could tear me limb from limb half the time."

"He wants you," Polly clarified. "Desire is violent, especially great desire that's been repressed too long. I've seen the way Evan looks at you. Believe me, it isn't hatred."

"He isn't a marrying man," Anna said wearily. "Even if he does want me, it isn't for keeps. I can't handle that kind of relationship. I'd hate myself."

"Is marrying a man you don't love any better?"

"Probably not," Anna had to admit. She put down her cup. "Randall and I are driving to Houston tomorrow for a party his parents are giving. We'll be late getting back. He wants to tell them about our engagement."

"All right. It's your life, Anna. I'll advise you, but I won't try to sway you again. You have to live with your own decisions, not mine."

Anna looked at the older woman quietly. "You're a terrific mother, did I ever tell you?"

Polly smiled gently. "Frequently. But I never tire of hearing it."

"I think I'll get to bed early tonight," Anna said. "I haven't been sleeping well lately."

"Do that, darling. Sleep tight."

"You, too."

But she didn't sleep. She lay awake, feeling over and over again the heat of Evan's mouth on her breast. She touched her bodice where the lace fell away and felt her body tauten at just the memory of his warm lips there. She shuddered, closing her eyes. She could hear his voice, whispering, seductive, teaching her how to touch him, to excite him, while he made her body sing with his mouth. She'd never dreamed she could feel so hungry, so wanton. But it had been new and frightening and embarrassing to be so intimate with him. She'd reacted badly. He'd gone away, as she'd asked, and he hadn't called or come back. Perhaps she'd really driven him away this time, and it might be for the best. Whatever her life was like with Randall, she wouldn't be at the mercy of her body, of needs she hadn't known she had.

Evan wasn't sleeping, either. He lay wide awake on his own bed, thinking of Anna, remembering the softness of her under his lips. That had been an error in judgment. He should have talked to her first, before he came on too strong and frightened her. He hadn't known she was so innocent that she felt insulted by the soft loveplay they'd shared. Under different circumstances, he could have taken her in his arms and explained it to her, gently coaxed her to give in to him. But he'd chosen a bad time, an impossible place. Next time, he'd have to be more cautious. But somehow he had to get her away from Randall before she married the man. Then what? What would he do about Anna? She was very innocent and the old fears still haunted him. What if he hurt her? What if his strength sent her running, as it had Louisa? Could he bear that?

He rolled over, closing his eyes. One step at a time, he thought bitterly. He'd done enough damage to her pride and her heart. Now he had to put it right. If he could.

Randall's parents lived in a middle-class suburban home in Houston, nothing really fancy, but nice. They were pleasant people. His father was a teacher, his mother a dietician, and they were kind to Anna. But she felt very much on display when their friends began to arrive, and it was almost a relief when Randall offered to go for more liquor later in the evening.

Anna went with him, despite his protests. The liquor store was in a bad part of town, he told her, and there was no drive-in. He'd have to leave her in the car.

She could lock it, she told him, laughing. He had nothing to worry about.

He gave in with obvious reluctance. Anna was wearing an expensive dress and a diamond pendant that Polly had bought for her. She looked as though she had money. But he couldn't talk her out of going with him, so he made her promise to stay in the car and keep the doors locked.

Ordinarily she would have done so. But a kitten wandering on the side street caught her attention. It was small and pitiful looking, and it headed right for the street.

There wasn't a soul in sight, and the parking lot was well lighted. She got out of the car and went after the kitten.

Unexpectedly it darted away and she followed, calling it. Her soft voice attracted the attention of a vagrant on the other side of the street. He saw the way she was dressed and assessed the shiny pendant around her neck and the glittery ring on her hand.

He was on her before she knew what had hit her. She fought like a tigress, but her struggling only enraged him and made him much more dangerous than he would have been if she'd let him have the diamond and the emerald ring.

She felt stark terror as his big fist connected with her face, and she screamed, but he kept hitting her. She couldn't even get away. He was an enormous man, heavyset and vicious, and by the time she finally blacked out, she tasted blood and felt as though he'd broken her to pieces...

Randall came back to the car and when he found it empty, he panicked. Dropping the bag of liquor on the hood of the car, he ran down the street, calling her. A shadow moved, and he went toward it hesitantly, just in time to see a man's shape move quickly away. There was a dark blob on the ground, and Randall knew all too well what it had to be.

He rushed to Anna's side, groaning as he saw her bleeding, bruised face. He examined her quickly, professionally. Her dress was torn but, thank God, the man hadn't raped her. He might have, if Randall hadn't come along when he had. As it was, he'd left with her jewelry. Her pulse was weak, but still there. There was blood in her hair from where she'd hit the pavement and she was almost surely concussed.

"Anna, can you hear me?" Randall asked huskily.

She didn't answer. She was unconscious.

He pulled out his penlight and examined her eyes quickly, grateful for his medical training. Definitely concussion, he thought, and that could be serious. He lifted her and struggled to get her into the car. Then he drove like a madman to the emergency room of the nearest hospital.

Harden was the only one at home when the telephone rang. He picked up the receiver, expecting a business call. But it was Polly Cochran on the other end of the line, half hysterical and all but incoherent.

"Slow down, Polly," he said curtly. "What is it?"

"It's Anna! Oh, God, I've got to get to Houston, Harden. I can't…I can't drive. Is Evan there?"

"No, he's flown to Dallas for a meeting." He didn't add that Evan had raised hell when he had to go, because his plans for the day were focused on something much more important than business, but he hadn't said what. He'd gone, with furious reluctance. "What's happened to Anna?"

"She's been mugged. She's in the hospital and badly hurt," Polly said shakily. "I have to…"

"I'll get Miranda and we'll be right over. You're at home?"

"Yes. Thank you!"

"No need. You'd do it for us." He hung up and went to find Miranda. Minutes later they picked Polly up at her house and headed toward Houston.

"She'll be all right, Polly," Miranda said gently, smiling reassuringly at her. "She's a strong girl."

"Oh, I hope so," Polly said huskily, fighting tears.

Anna was in the intensive care unit when they got to the hospital, attached to life support systems, her breathing labored, her eyes closed. Her face was a mass of bruises and cuts, one eye almost swollen shut. Randall came out of the unit to talk to them in the hall.

"She's had a bad time of it," he said quietly. "The concussion is what worries us most. For the rest, it's just bruises and cuts, and she'll heal."

"She wasn't raped?" Polly asked through her teeth.

Randall shook his head. "I got to her in time to frighten the man off." He sighed wearily. "Oh, God, I'm so sorry. It's my fault. We went out to get some more liquor for the party, and I told her to stay in the car, so that she'd be safe. I still don't understand what made her get out of it."

"Why did you take her with you?" Polly wailed.

"She insisted," Randall said helplessly.

If it had been Evan, she'd have stayed at home, Polly thought angrily. Evan would have protected her. But she didn't say it. Randall looked broken up enough as it was.

They went into the intensive care unit and Polly sat beside her daughter, holding her hand. She had to get well. She had to!

It was morning before Harden and Miranda got home. Polly had refused to leave, so Harden had promised to return later in the day with some things she needed. He told Donald and Theodora what was going on, then grabbed a few hours sleep. He got up early and did what he needed to do on the ranch before he went to Polly's house and filled an overnight case for her. Then he drove back to Houston.

It was suppertime when he returned. He was worn and haggard. Evan was home, but he'd been out most of the day and had just joined the family. Nobody had told him yet.

Harden didn't know that. He clapped Evan on the shoulder. "I'm sorry about Anna," he said quietly.

Evan shrugged. "One of those things," he said curtly and turned away.

Harden was shocked by Evan's lack of feeling, but perhaps he was still raw from her engagement and hiding it.

Harden sat down and waited for Theodora to say grace. While they ate, Evan talked about the meeting and what he'd learned.

Miranda had felt nauseated, so she was late getting downstairs. She'd been asleep when Harden came home, so he hadn't wanted to wake her. He smiled at her as she joined them, lifting his face for her soft kiss before she eased into the chair beside him, her pregnancy delightfully obvious.

"How is she?" she asked gently.

"There's no change," Harden said heavily. "I promised Polly I'd drive back up tomorrow, so that she won't be completely alone. She's tried to contact Duke, but he's out of the country. They expect him back tomorrow. I hope to God…"

"Do they have any idea who did it?" Theodora asked quietly.

"Not yet," Harden said. "They won't, unless he tries to fence the jewelry. That's a long shot, too."

"Maybe not," Miranda interrupted, aware of Evan's sudden interest. "That emerald solitaire would stand out, wouldn't it?"

"So it would," Harden agreed.

"What the hell are you talking about?" Evan asked. "Anna has an emerald solitaire."

"She did have," Harden said. "It was stolen."

"How?"

Harden sat very still. He glanced around the table, from Donald and Jo Anne to Theodora. "Hasn't anybody told him yet?" he asked softly.

"There wasn't time," Theodora said gently. She grimaced as she looked at Evan. "And I didn't quite know how—"

"Tell me what?" Evan ground out.

"Anna's in the hospital in Houston," Harden said quietly. "She was attacked and badly hurt. She's in a coma."

He hated doing that to Evan in front of the others. He alone had a good idea of how Evan really felt about Anna, and it was like stripping his pride naked.

Evan handled it well, though. Except for his sudden pallor and a certain awkwardness about his movements when he stood up, he looked perfectly normal.

"Let's go," he told Harden.

Harden knew when not to argue. He kissed Miranda. "Don't wait up. I'll be back when I can."

"Drive carefully," she said, smiling.

He nodded toward the others and followed Evan out.

"Give me a cigarette," the bigger man said when they were headed toward Houston in Harden's car.

"You don't smoke."

"I just started."

He handed Evan his cigarettes and matches. "I hate corrupting you. Next you'll want a drink."

"I already do. Tell me how it happened."

"I'd rather not."

"Why?"

"Because you're volatile enough already."

"It was that damned doctor, wasn't it? He let her out of his sight."

"In a nutshell, yes, but he did tell her to stay in the car. She got out, God knows why, and was attacked for her jewelry. Apparently she put up a hell of a fight, but judging from the beating she took, he was big and mean."

Evan cursed solidly for five minutes, going from anger to rage to murderous fury. Harden didn't try to stop him.

He knew exactly how he'd feel if it was Miranda in that hospital room.

"What are her chances?" he asked finally, almost choking as he drew on the cigarette.

"Fifty-fifty. We'll have to wait and see."

"Does she want to live, do you think?" he asked, his voice haunted. "I've hurt her, Harden. I've really hurt her."

"It wasn't your fault that you wanted her out of your life," he reminded the other man.

"But I didn't," Evan said miserably. "I was afraid I might hurt her. After Louisa…"

"We've had this conversation before. Anna isn't Louisa. You might have given her a chance."

"Yes. I know." He took another draw from the cigarette. "I was planning to. I thought I still might be able to take her away from Randall, if I tried."

"Glory be! You got intelligent!"

"I got desperate," he said huskily. "I had the sweetest taste of her you could imagine at the art gallery two days ago. I haven't slept since. I want her until my heart aches."

Harden glanced at his hard, set face. "I know how that feels," he said gently. "I hope it works out for you."

"I hope she lives," Evan said dully. "That's all I want, for the moment. That, and to kill the man who put her in that bed."

Harden didn't say a word. He understood.

An hour later Evan was allowed into the intensive care unit. He cursed silently at the sight of her poor, hurt face. He should have never forced her out of his life. He'd brought this on her, by letting Randall take her away without a fight. He couldn't bear it if she died.

He sat down by the bed and slid her slender, cool hand between his big warm ones.

"Anna," he whispered.

She didn't stir, but he could have sworn he saw her eyelashes flicker, just a hair.

"Anna, it's me. It's Evan. Can you hear me, baby?"

The endearment got a reaction. Her fingers moved slightly in the cradle of his hands.

"Yes, you can hear me, can't you, little one?" he asked softly. He got to his feet and bent down, so that there was no danger that anyone passing by the open door could hear him. "Do you remember what we did together in the art gallery, Anna?" he whispered, his warm breath stirring the soft blond hair at her ear. "Do you remember how, and where, I kissed you?"

She made a soft sound and her eyebrows jerked.

His lips brushed her earlobe. His teeth gently closed on it. "I loved the feel of your breast under my mouth, Anna," he whispered. "I want it again."

She moaned. He lifted his head, his eyes glittering with triumph as she began to move her head.

"That's it," he coaxed. "That's it, little one, come back. Come back to me."

Seconds later her eyes opened and focused on him. She grimaced and they closed again and she shivered.

He pushed the nurse's call button. When the nurse arrived, before she could speak, he said, "She's conscious."

That was all it took. He was escorted out into the hall while a team of white-coated people marched into her room.

"She came to," he told Polly, smiling. "She'll be fine."

"But, how?" Polly asked, hugging him, laughing. "What did you say to her?"

He cleared his throat and looked uncomfortable. "I just talked to her," he said evasively. He scowled suddenly, glancing around. "Where's Randall?" he asked.

"He's staying with his parents," Polly said. "He was tired, so he went to get some sleep."

"With her here?" Evan asked, outraged.

Harden caught his arm and pulled him aside while the doctor came out and spoke with Polly.

"You're waving a flag," Harden cautioned.

"I can't help it," Evan raged. "Damn it, doesn't he care?"

"Not the way you do," the other man replied quietly. "Or isn't that already obvious?"

Evan ran a rough hand through his hair. "She flinched. She looked at me and flinched. If she didn't hate me, she probably does now."

"She's disoriented and in pain," Harden replied. "Give it time."

"Time," Evan said on a heavy sigh. "Yes."

He pursed his lips. "What did you say to her?"

Evan actually flushed. He gave Harden a cold glare and went to listen to what the doctor was saying.

Anna was going to be all right, the doctor told them, but there would more than likely be some emotional trauma and she'd need counseling. Being overpowered and beaten by the man could affect her drastically. He was a big man, too, the doctor had added, and very strong. He glanced at Evan ruefully and said flatly that she might find Evan's presence frightening and even a little intimidating until she had time to recover from her ordeal.

Evan listened, but he didn't leave. If Randall wasn't going to assume his responsibility for Anna, Evan certainly was. He wouldn't go away and leave her, and he said so. The doctor only smiled.

Polly was grateful for Evan's company in the days that followed, because Randall had to go back to work. He walked wide around Evan, feeling more guilty than ever when the big man glared at him. Anna loved Evan, and Randall hated standing in the way of her happiness. His original reason for wanting to marry her had begun to disturb him more and more as he realized how unhappy Anna had been. They'd been friends, and he missed her old, bubbling personality. Now, more than ever, he wanted her to be happy. He knew he couldn't give her that. But Evan could. He was leaving the field clear for the man she really loved. When she was well again, he'd break off the engagement, as gently as he could, and hope that things would work out for her.

Evan didn't know about the rationale, so he spent the better part of the day cursing Randall for all he was worth. He cursed even more when Anna suddenly refused to see him.

He couldn't accept that. He waited until Polly went to get herself a cup of coffee in the hospital canteen, then he calmly walked into Anna's room and sat down in the chair beside her bed.

She stiffened at his approach, and her eyes grew huge. He knew she must be connecting his size with that of her assailant, but it was more than he could do to leave her now.

"Don't be afraid of me," he said quietly, searching her blackened eyes. "I'm not going to hurt you. Not ever."

She seemed to relax a little, but her posture was still rigid, and she didn't take her eyes off him.

"Where's Randall?" she asked, her voice slurred because of the medicine they were giving her.

"You can forget Randall," he said shortly. "Because the last thing in the world you're going to do is marry him."

# *Chapter 7*

Anna was certain that she couldn't possibly have heard him right. "What?" she faltered.

"I said, you're not marrying Randall," he replied matter-of-factly. He glanced at the tray they'd brought her for lunch. "You aren't eating. Do you want them to put those tubes back in and feed you intravenously?"

"I'm not hungry," she said, dazed.

He got up and uncovered the food dishes, his dark eyes glaring at her. "You've lost enough weight."

"I'm a big girl," she muttered.

"Hmm," he agreed absently, letting his eyes fall to the thrust of her breasts under the thin hospital gown. He smiled gently. "In places."

She flushed and her breath drew in.

Evan cocked an eyebrow. "Shocked? You remember how I pulled you back, don't you, little one?" he asked softly. "What I reminded you of."

She swallowed, feeling trapped and nervous of him, painfully shy. She lowered her eyes to the white sheet.

He wouldn't have that. He touched her bruised chin very gently and lifted her face to his, searching her eyes in a tense silence. He remembered then, vividly, how she'd reacted to the intimate caress, what she'd thought. He smiled gently. "Anna, what I did to you wasn't meant to make you feel cheap," he said, his voice deep and tender.

"I…I know, now," she said hesitantly, without adding that Polly had explained it to her. "It frightened me," she whispered.

"Yes, and I think I know why." He bent, his eyes falling to her soft lips. He brushed them gently with his. "Desire can be frightening. The way I want you scares the hell out of me. Now more than ever."

She trembled, her eyes closing as his lips touched hers with lazy expertise. Her hand went to his arm, the nails digging into the huge muscle, scraping gently as he played with her mouth.

"Oh, Evan, you shouldn't," she moaned helplessly at his lips. "I'm engaged…"

His mouth pressed down on hers hungrily, driving all thoughts of Randall and honor right out of her mind. She cried out, both hands trembling at his nape, curling into it while he forced her mouth open and his tongue thrust hungrily into it.

Her helpless shudder and the sounds she made under his mouth brought him back to sanity. She was weak and hurt. He had no right to torment her.

He lifted his head slowly, his eyes opening to search hers. "I'm sorry," he whispered. "But I needed that. Here, stop shaking, little one, or they'll think I'm torturing you."

"Aren't you?" she whispered back, her voice shaken.

His eyes darkened, his jaw went taut. "It felt like that, didn't it?" he asked huskily. "I wanted so much more than your lips, Anna." His eyes went to her breasts, where her taut nipples betrayed the emotion he'd summoned up in her. "Do they want my mouth on them?" he whispered. "With no fabric in the way to dull the warmth and moistness when I take you inside it?"

She moaned hoarsely.

He caught his breath, standing up abruptly. "God, I'm sorry!" he ground out.

She turned her head and found herself looking down the broad sweep of his chest and shoulder to the thick belt that held up his jeans. And then at the evidence of his uncontrollable response to their quick passion.

"Yes, I want you," he said curtly, following her eyes to his body. "I can't hide it, can I?"

She bit her lower lip, struggling for words.

"No need to agonize over it," he murmured, going back to the plates on her tray as he moved it across her lap. "It will subside eventually," he added with rueful humor.

He made it sound matter-of-fact, and he didn't seem to be embarrassed that she saw him like that. She watched his face as he undid the lids from the plates.

"It doesn't embarrass you?" she asked in a whisper.

"Not particularly." He laughed shortly, glancing down at her. "In fact, it's a welcome change."

"I don't understand."

"Don't you?" He laid the lids aside. "It doesn't happen with other women lately," he said, turning to face her. "In fact, I can't make it happen with anyone else. Only you."

Her eyes spoke volumes, half questioning, half jealous.

He nodded. "That's right. I tried. I went to Denver on business after I'd kissed you that day in the gallery. I deliberately came on to one of the party girls I met there and took her upstairs with me. We drank and watched television, and I sent her away, because despite her beauty and her obvious expertise, I couldn't even pretend to be interested."

"You…were…?"

"The word is impotent," he said quietly. "Ironic, isn't it? All I have to do is look at you, and I'm so aroused I can't even hold a fork."

He drew her attention to it, to the fine tremor of his big hand as he dipped the fork into a creamy chicken dish. She hated the thought of him with another woman, even if it did make her feel warm all over to realize that he only wanted her.

"Open up," he said gently, lifting the food to her mouth.

"But, you don't have to do that," she protested. All the same, she opened her mouth and let him slide the forkful in.

"Yes, I do," he replied gently, searching her poor, bruised face. "I've hurt you more than I ever meant to. But that's over. I'm going to take the most exquisite care of you from now on, Anna."

Because he felt sorry for her. That, and desire. She could have cried.

"But, Randall," she whispered.

His eyes flashed at her from under thick brown eyebrows. "Randall can go to hell. He never should have taken you to that liquor store. And you haven't yet said why you got out of the car in the first place."

"There was a kitten," she said, her eyes softening with the memory. "It was lost and heading for the street."

His heart turned over. At that moment, he loved her with such passion that his body could barely contain it. He wanted to throw the tray aside and come down beside her on the bed.

She lifted her eyes, puzzled by his silence, and saw the vicious heat of his gaze. Her face froze.

"What is it?" he rasped.

"That look," she said, averting her gaze. "You looked as if you hated me."

He reached down and turned her face back to his. "That look is a raging desire that I can only just control," he said tightly. "Yes," he added when she stared at him. "It's every bit as violent as hatred, but I assure you, it isn't. And there's no need to be afraid of it, or me. Nothing is going to happen, Anna, least of all while you're lying there bruised and broken."

"I'm not afraid of you," she said gently.

"Aren't you?" he asked curtly. "The doctor said that you were going to have some emotional trauma because of what happened. The man was about my size, he said."

Her eyes swept over him softly. "Yes," she agreed. "But he was a cold, brutal stranger who wanted my jewelry."

His heart leapt. "I see."

He lifted another forkful of chicken to her mouth, taking his time, feeding her as gently as if she'd been a child.

"My eye hurts," she said when he finished and moved the tray away.

"I don't doubt it. You've got a shiner."

She managed a smile. Her face hurt when it moved. "I can tell people I was in a brawl."

"You gave him a few bruises, I hear," he said, hating the thought of some man beating her.

"A few bites, too," she muttered angrily. "He could have just taken the jewelry, he didn't have to…to hit me like that!"

Evan was vibrating with equal anger. She looked up and saw his face. It calmed her down.

The painkillers made her oddly comfortable with him, as if she didn't have to fight her feelings or avoid personal questions.

"Evan, can I ask you something very personal?" she asked after a minute.

He was lighting a cigarette. He turned back to her, his dark hair falling roguishly onto his broad forehead, his jeans taut across his powerful legs as he leaned back against the wall beside the window and crossed them.

"Shoot," he invited.

"You're smoking!" she exclaimed.

His big shoulders rose and fell. "Just as well I couldn't leave you long enough to go to a bar, or I'd be drinking, too," he said.

"But why?"

"Because I was worried, of course," he said, staring at her as if she were demented. "Polly spoke to your father this morning, by the way," he added. "He returned to the States last night and got the message she'd left for him the night you were brought in. He's on his way out from Atlanta now."

"Daddy?" She smiled, delighted. "I haven't seen him for years."

"I know. Polly's pretty nervous herself."

"I wish they could make up," she murmured. "Neither of them wants anyone else, but they can't live together."

"Your father will get tired of wandering someday and come home," he told her. "Polly, I imagine, will be waiting." He stared at her, curls of smoke drifting up from his cigarette. "What did you want to ask me?"

"Oh. That." She studied his dark, unsmiling face. "You've been so different lately," she murmured. "Not the same man you were."

"How was I?"

"Lighthearted," she recalled. "Carefree and playful. You've changed. Is it because of Nina?"

"What do you think, baby?"

She blushed at the endearment, remembering how and when he'd said it.

"Was that what you wanted to know?"

She drew in a slow breath. "No." She studied her clasped hands. One was scraped raw where she'd fallen to the pavement during her struggle with her assailant. The experience had been terrifying, and she'd had nightmares since, but when Evan was around, she didn't think about it.

"Well?" he asked impatiently.

"I don't think I can."

He moved closer to the bed. "There is nothing, absolutely nothing, you can't ask me," he told her quietly.

"Even about...about that girl who said you hurt her?" she asked, repeating the gossip Polly had once told her.

He froze. His face stiffened as all his fears came back to torment him.

She looked up and winced. "I'm sorry. Evan, I'm sorry!"

He met her worried eyes and took a deep breath. "It was a long time ago," he said dully.

"And you don't want to talk about it," she said. "I shouldn't have said anything."

His brows drew together. "What did you want to know about it? How I hurt her?"

She went scarlet and dropped her eyes.

He laughed bitterly. "Is that what you think, Anna?" he asked on an expelled breath. "That I get my kicks from being cruel in bed?"

Her hands tightened together until the knuckles went white. "No!"

"What if I do?" he persisted, angry that she could think

of him that way. He remembered his own roughness with
her when he'd kissed her, and realized that he might have
given her a foundation for her assumptions. He moved
closer to the bed, his eyes glittery with temper. "What if I
like it?"

She ground her teeth together. "I know you're not like
that," she said stubbornly.

"Do you?" he leaned down, his eyes looking straight
into hers, making her heart jump and run. "I bit you," he
whispered. "Do you remember where?"

Her body trembled with the memory, her breasts going
hard-tipped, betraying her. "Yes," she whispered. "But it…
didn't hurt."

"It wasn't supposed to," he said quietly. His eyes searched
hers. "You've never made love at all, have you? Not even
with Randall."

"It always seemed so intimate," she replied nervously.
"Almost distasteful."

"But not with me?"

Her lips parted as her gaze fell helplessly to his hard
mouth, and she remembered how it felt to kiss him with
her whole heart and have him kiss her back in that hungry,
expert way. "Nothing could ever seem distasteful with you,"
she managed weakly, too shattered to lie, even to save her
pride.

His hand pressed gently against her cheek, his thumb
rubbing softly over her swollen lips. He bent and brushed
his nose against hers.

"Louisa was very small," he whispered. "And as
innocent as you are. We were going to become engaged,
and I wanted her very badly. So I took her back to my
apartment and undressed her. Then I pulled off my clothes
and turned around…and she went white in the face."

Her eyes lifted to his, startled.

He nodded grimly. "She was half your size. She knew nothing of sex except what she'd gleaned from her romance novels. I was crazy to have her and I didn't realize how frightened she was. I thought I could coax her into my arms. For a few seconds I thought she was mine. Then I lost control, and she couldn't get free. She fought me and screamed. I came to my senses just as she fell off the bed and hurt her ribs." He stood up, his face pale. "She said some things…" He turned away, hiding the look in his eyes. "Anyway, that was my first and last experience of virgins. Since then I've avoided them like the plague."

"If you loved her enough to marry her, it must have been a terrible blow to your pride," she said quietly, understanding now his reluctance to become involved with her.

"It was." He sighed heavily and glanced at her gentle face, at its soft flush. "She'd never seen a naked man before, much less one as obviously aroused as I was." His eyes narrowed at her embarrassment. "You haven't either, have you, Anna?"

"No," she confessed huskily.

"She left Jacobsville soon afterward. The last I heard she was married to some insurance agent and had two children." He laughed bitterly. "Maybe he had the good sense to get her drunk and turn the lights out first."

Her eyes widened. "You didn't have the lights out?"

She looked horrified. In spite of himself, he began to laugh. "Oh, my God, you don't think people only make love at night, in the dark?"

"Don't they?" she asked, trying to imagine how embarrassing it would be to lie down with a man like that in broad daylight.

He sat down heavily in the chair beside the bed. "Remind

me to give you a copy of the Kamasutra for Christmas," he said ruefully.

She knew what the book was, even if she didn't own one. "Evan!"

"All right, keep your inhibitions." He pursed his lips as he flicked ashes into the ashtray on her bedside table. "Not that you had many, in the gallery that day," he remarked softly. "Or any other time I've touched you."

Her heart was going crazy. "You shouldn't talk to me like this," she began.

"Because of the beloved physician?" he asked sarcastically.

"Because…it's not decent," she said uneasily.

He just shook his head. "Baby, you are a case," he murmured. "So many repressions."

"Don't make fun of me," she said curtly. "It's no sin not to sleep around."

His eyebrows lifted. "Did I say it was?"

"You said I was repressed," she muttered.

His lips tugged into a reluctant smile. "Repressed, but passionate," he replied. "All you need is a few lessons."

She swallowed. "Randall can give them to me."

"That'll be the day," he said flatly. "I told you, consider your engagement broken. Randall's not getting you. Any lessons you get from now on will be from me."

"You don't want me!" she burst out.

"And you know better," he said quietly.

She glared at him in a frustrated fury. "You can't build a relationship on desire."

"I agree." He leaned back in the chair, his eyes dark and possessive. "But you can build one on love."

"I love Randall," she choked.

He only smiled. "No, you don't," he said softly. "You love me."

"You don't want me to," she replied miserably, not bothering to deny it. She lay back against the pillows and closed her eyes wearily. "I'm sleepy."

"Rest is the best thing for you. I'll go and find Polly." He put out his cigarette and adjusted the pillow under her head, pulling the sheet up to her breasts. The back of his knuckles brushed the tip of one and it went immediately taut.

She blushed, but he didn't tease her about it. If anything, his face grew more solemn.

"When you're out of here," he said, "we're going to start spending some time together."

"You don't have to do that," she murmured.

"I know. I want to." He bent and brushed his mouth gently across her forehead. "My poor bruised baby," he whispered. "I'm sorry he hurt you."

Tears threatened at his tenderness. He'd been every way with her, from teasing to cold to passionate, but he'd never been tender before.

"Nina won't like it," she said unsteadily. "And neither will Randall," she added.

"Neither of them matters," he said, dismissing them. He brushed his lips softly against hers. "Go to sleep. I'll be here when you wake up."

"But you don't want me around," she whispered as she began to doze. "You keep throwing Nina at me to prove it."

His face went rigid with self-contempt. "Every man's entitled to one stupid mistake."

"She's very pretty." She sighed.

"Go to sleep," he said gruffly.

She did, her last conscious thought was that he sounded angry about something, but she was too sleepy to wonder what.

When she woke again, a tall man with graying blond

hair and blue eyes was sitting in the chair where Evan had been, gravely concerned.

"Papa!" she exclaimed, and held out her arms.

He went into them with rough laughter, hugging her warmly. "And here I sat, worried to death about the kind of reception I'd get."

"Don't be silly. You're my dad. I love you."

"I'm sorry I wasn't here sooner," he said bitterly. "I was out of the country. I didn't know until last night. How are you?" He stood up, studying her. "They said you were badly concussed."

"I was, but I'm much better. Just a little battered."

"So I see. And the man, the one who did it?"

"They haven't caught him yet, but they may be able to trace him through the jewelry he took."

"If he was a junkie, that's not likely," he said heavily. "They have a network all their own for fencing goods. My poor little girl!"

"I'll be all right."

"No thanks to your so-called fiancé," he growled. "What possessed you to let yourself be talked into marrying that wimp?" he demanded. "I thought you were head over heels in love with Evan Tremayne!"

"She is," came a deep, amused drawl from the doorway as Evan sauntered in, carrying two cups of coffee. Anna flushed, and he grinned. "Still take it black, Duke?"

Duke Cochran chuckled, rising to take the cup from Evan and shake hands. "Yes, I still do. How are you?"

"Tired." He glanced past him at Anna, who was pale but looked at least a little better. "We all are. It's been a long week."

"I know. I'm sorry I wasn't here."

"Couldn't be helped."

"Yes, it could," Duke said angrily, running a restless

hand through his hair. "I'm never around when I'm needed. Polly's right, my family's only been an afterthought, hasn't it, sweetheart?" he asked Anna.

"It hasn't," she disagreed, her eyes soft. "You just can't settle down. I understand. Most men love their freedom," she added without daring to look at Evan.

"Freedom can cost too much sometimes," Duke replied tersely.

"Amen," Evan said under his breath.

Polly came in the door and stopped, her hand going to her throat as she looked into blue eyes she hadn't seen for two long years. "Duke," she whispered.

"Hello, pumpkin," he said, smiling hesitantly. "Surprise, it's really me."

"You look…"

"If you say marvelous," Duke threatened dryly, "I'll smack you. Come here, woman, and give me a kiss. I've gone hungry too long already!"

"Oh, you!"

Polly blushed, but she went to him, lifting her face for a kiss that, when it came, made the other occupants of the room feel briefly like intruders. Polly was breathless when Duke let her go.

He chuckled huskily at her expression. "Worth the wait, wasn't it, pumpkin?" he asked. "Glad to see me? God, I'm glad to see you! You look more beautiful every year."

"You flatterer." Polly faltered. "You always did have the devil's own charm."

"Doesn't he look great?" Anna asked her mother.

"Yes, he does," Polly had to admit. He was tanned and slender, no beer belly or excess weight. She averted her eyes to Anna. "But you don't. How are you, darling?"

"Better," Anna said doggedly. "When can I come home?"

"Your doctor said tomorrow, if you feel like it," Polly

said, beaming. "You'll have to take it easy, of course, and they do want you to have some counseling," she added.

"We can talk about that when I get home," Anna replied. "I really don't feel that traumatized."

"You save that for when you're asleep," Evan said quietly. "You've been having nightmares. Painful ones, judging by the way you thrash around."

"He's right," Polly agreed. "Maybe the trauma is buried in your subconscious, but it's still there."

Anna grimaced. "If I'd only stayed in the car like Randall told me to." She sighed. "Speaking of Randall, has anyone seen him today?"

"He phoned," Polly said. "But he's got exams and he can't come to see you. He asked if you needed anything."

"What a loving fiancé," Evan said with bitter mockery, his dark eyes narrow and cruel.

"You stop that," Anna muttered. "Exams are very important to him."

"More important than you are, obviously," he shot back.

She glared at him. "My personal life is none of your business!"

"It is, when you do stupid things like agreeing to marry fools!"

"Now, now," Polly chided, getting between them. "Anna needs rest. So do you, Evan. You haven't slept more than an hour or two since the day after it happened."

"Good suggestion," Duke seconded. He clapped Evan on the shoulder. "Thanks for the coffee."

Evan was reluctant to leave, but he was feeling the strain. He glanced at Anna, grimaced and let himself be persuaded out the door by Duke.

Polly smiled at her daughter. "He's very antagonistic

about Randall, I'm afraid," she mused. "He's said some things I won't even repeat to you."

"Randall is none of his business," she said doggedly.

"He won't believe that. He's very possessive, isn't he?" she asked with a twinkle in her eyes. "He hasn't left you since they brought you in, except to sleep."

She knew that. It warmed her, somehow. Randall's behavior was unexpected. He had compassion, and she knew he cared about her, but he was deliberately staying away. She couldn't help but wonder why.

"Evan knows how I feel," she told Polly. "Do you think it's some game he's playing, trying to turn me against Randall? Or is it a case of dog in the manger?" She sighed miserably. "Oh, Mama, he just feels sorry for me, that's all it is. Once I'm well, he'll take off like a rocket, you wait and see."

"Evan is deep," Polly said. "Let the future take care of itself. Right now, you concentrate on getting well."

"All right. It's nice to have Papa home, isn't it?"

Polly sighed with more feeling than she realized. "Oh, yes. It is, indeed."

Anna didn't say another word, but she smiled. She refused to let herself think about Evan's odd behavior and the hungry way he'd kissed her. Perhaps he enjoyed the feeling of power it gave him to know that she cared so deeply for him. About his own feelings, he'd said nothing. For all she knew, he could be planning to marry Nina. She didn't recognize the man he'd become lately. Of course, she thought dazedly, he'd never treated her like a woman until very recently. A man was one way with friends and family, but a totally different way with a woman he desired. She flushed remembering how helplessly he wanted her.

Could it be just desire driving him? She knew men could fool themselves about their emotions when their glands were involved. She didn't dare trust anything Evan said or did right now, while she was flat on her back. If it was only pity, or even only desire, she couldn't risk breaking her heart on him again.

## Chapter 8

Randall came to see Anna an hour later, looking remorseful and quiet.

"I hope you're better," he said, sitting down beside her. He searched her bruised face and grimaced. "I feel terrible about what happened."

"I know. But it really wasn't your fault," she said gently. "I got out of the car."

"Why?"

She told him, ruefully, and he just shook his head.

"How did exams go?"

"Well, I hope," he said, smiling just faintly as he looked at her. "My heart wasn't in it. I was worried about you."

"I'll be all right," she assured him.

He crossed his legs and leaned back. "I see that Evan's very much in residence."

She flushed a little and averted her eyes. "Yes."

He smiled. "Don't be embarrassed. I've always known

how you felt about him. This engagement of ours isn't going to work, Anna. You can't marry me when you're in love with someone else."

Her eyes were sad as they met his. "I guess not."

"We were friends," he reminded her. "I like the girl you were—the impulsive, happy, bubbling girl who played jokes and never stopped laughing. I don't like the middle-aged woman I've made you into."

"But, Randall, you haven't!" she protested.

He held up a hand, silencing her. "Probably some of it was because of Evan, but being engaged to me hasn't improved you. I want you to be happy again. I want us to be friends again." He grimaced. "I don't know that I'm ready to settle down yet. Evan was right. If I'd cared enough, I couldn't have gone out with anyone except you. And if you cared enough, you'd have been furious."

She couldn't argue, because he was right. She sat up against the pillows, drawing her knees up so that she could rest her hands on them. "Yes."

"Besides," he said with an amused smile, "Evan just got through telling me I couldn't have you."

Her eyes flashed. "He has no right…!"

"I'm afraid he thinks he does," Randall mused. "You can argue the point with him."

"He just feels sorry for me," she said heavily, staring at her slender hands. "Once I'm back on my feet again, he'll be lying awake nights trying to think of ways to discourage me, just the way he used to."

Randall didn't think so, but he didn't argue with her.

"I'm sorry about my beautiful engagement ring," she said.

"It was insured," he said easily. "I'm only sorry about the way you lost it. Poor little thing."

"I'm not little, and I'm getting stronger every day. When

I'm well, I'm signing up for karate," she said angrily. "I'll learn to pulverize muggers."

"That's a good idea," he agreed. "Self-defense should be part of every woman's repertoire."

They talked for a long time, and when Randall left, promising to keep in touch, it was as if a weight had been lifted from her head. The engagement had been a mistake, but she couldn't regret it. Randall had saved her pride after Evan's vicious rejection.

Evan had gone home to change his clothes, simmering with fury because he'd encountered Randall in the corridor. He'd sent the man off with a cold warning, but it might be too little too late. He was sure that Anna loved him, but he'd treated her pretty badly. She might very well marry Randall out of desperation. He had to stop her, but how?

He could, of course, marry her himself. His face went blank as he considered that possibility for the first time. Marriage had never been one of his personal priorities, but he was crazy about Anna and he wanted her. They could have children. He drew in a slow breath. The thought appealed to him. Anna, children, a home of his own. Anna in his bed… His heart began to thunder in his chest as he considered marriage and found that it wasn't the terror he'd once thought. His fear of hurting her would be an obstacle, of course, as would her fear of big men. But in time, they could work that out. If she'd have him now.

He groaned inwardly at his own stupidity in turning away from her. She didn't trust him because he'd hurt her so badly, rejected her not only fiercely but in public. He must have savaged her pride. After their argument the night before, he wasn't sure he could even get into her room without a struggle. She might rush right into Randall's arms for protection. The thought made him miserable all the way back to Jacobsville.

"How is she?" Harden asked almost as soon as Evan got in the door of the Tremayne house. Because of Evan's absence, and that of Jo Anne and Donald, Harden and Miranda were staying with Theodora to help with ranch business.

"Better," Evan said tersely, tossing his hat on the hall table. "Her fiancé showed up just as I left."

Harden lifted an eyebrow. "I thought you approved of her engagement."

"So did I."

He stared at the older man quietly, his blue eyes seeing the lines in Evan's face, the tautness. "You look like hell."

"It's been touch and go for a while. She's only just beginning to pick up. How are things here?"

"We're handling them just fine. I assume you're going back?"

"I'll have to," Evan said curtly, his dark eyes stormy, "or she may let herself be talked into a hospital wedding by that pill-pushing wimp."

Harden had to bite back a grin. "He's not bad."

"Not when he's a hundred miles away from Anna," Evan agreed.

Harden's blue eyes searched the other man's face. "You said that she was too young. That you didn't want her. But I don't think you realize how you've changed since Anna hasn't been around." He shook his head slowly. "Honest to God, I hardly know you these days."

"Anna said that," he admitted. He jammed his big hands into his pockets with a rough curse. "She'll be even more fragile after what's happened to her, and I don't know how I'm going to handle my own doubts. But leaving her to the mercies of young Dr. Randall isn't something I can live with. I'm not perfect, but she'd be better off with me. At least I won't drive her around strange cities at night hunting muggers."

Harden had to bite back laughter at the disgust in that deep voice. "I thought you were afraid of your own strength."

Evan gazed at him evenly. "I was. I am. I don't know how I'll handle that, either." His big shoulders lifted. "She makes me shake like a boy. God knows I'll probably send her running when things heat up, but I can't push her away again. Not now."

"You may underestimate Anna's feelings," Harden reminded him. "And Anna's no shrinking violet. If she loves you, everything will be all right."

"She loves me, all right," Evan said quietly. "That's the only thing I'm still sure of. But she thinks I just feel sorry for her, and Randall's handy." He looked up. "I told him he couldn't have her."

Harden smiled. "Good for you. But have you told Anna?"

"I will." He moved into the living room and went to speak to his mother before he caught up on business and started back to Houston.

It was almost dark when Evan returned to Anna's hospital room. She'd been sure he wasn't coming back, but surprisingly, he showed up with a huge white teddy bear under one arm. He slung it beside her on the bed, his dark eyes accusing.

"What…!" Anna exclaimed, her eyes beaming as she lifted the enormous, soft bear. She'd been ready for a fight, but he'd stolen her thunder. The bear was beautiful, and it touched her that he'd cared even enough to bring her a present.

"His name's Hubert," he told her irritably. "You can be engaged to him."

She laughed, cuddling the bear beside her. "He's beautiful," she said shyly, knowing that she'd treasure it for the rest of her life. "Thank you."

He shrugged. His eyes narrowed. "What did Randall want?"

Her eyebrows jerked up. "To see how I was, of course."

"Did you break the engagement?" he persisted.

"No, I did not," she shot at him. That was true. Randall had broken it, but her pride wouldn't let her tell Evan.

He moved to her side and bent over her, his dark face threatening as his gaze fell to her mouth. "What was that?"

The closeness made her dizzy. He was wearing a yellow knit shirt with tight-fitting jeans. He was enormous, lean and muscular and he smelled of expensive cologne. His head was bare, dark brown hair neatly combed, his face freshly shaven. He was so sensuous that her mouth ached for his, but she wasn't about to be taken in a second time.

"My engagement is none of your business," she said stubbornly. He was too close. She clutched the bear for protection, knowing all too well that he could touch her and knock every one of her barriers spinning. He probably knew it. She was too green to hide the effect he had on her.

"Suppose I make it my business?" he asked quietly, holding her gaze. "Suppose I tell you that I'm jealous as hell and I don't want another man's hands on you?"

Her heart ran away, but she wasn't going to be taken in. "I've been hurt and you feel sorry for me," she said shortly. "You don't have to throw out your arms and profess love eternal just because I got mugged, Evan."

His face colored angrily. "It isn't pity."

"What else could you ever feel for me?" she asked bitterly.

He drew in his breath sharply and stood up, his hands jammed deep in his pockets. He'd been living on his nerves for too long, he supposed, because her harsh question made him sick inside. His self-confidence took a nosedive. Apparently she'd decided not to believe anything he told her from now on. How could he convince her that he'd had a sincere change of heart about her place in his life?

"That's right," she muttered darkly, "stand there and glare at me. At least that would be honest."

"What's gotten into you?" he asked flatly.

"I've seen the light, dear man," she returned. "Maybe I've even grown up a little as well. I've just gone off hero worship, Evan."

His hands clenched in his pockets, but his face gave nothing away. "Is that all it was?"

"I'm nineteen," she reminded him. "Too young for undying love and commitment, isn't that what you thought?"

His face tautened with strain. "It wasn't just your age."

"Then what was it?"

"Louisa," he said quietly.

She remembered what he'd told her about the other woman and her face softened. She could only imagine the scars that the experience had left on him. Her eyes fell to the bear and she stroked the soft fake fur gently.

"If she'd really loved you, Evan, nothing would have frightened her," she said, her voice subdued.

"Are you sure?"

He sounded mocking, cynical. She glanced at him, her eyes faintly adoring. He looked so tired. "I would have been glad to prove it to you, once," she said.

His eyes flashed in a face like stone. "Think so?" he

asked on a hard laugh. "You don't even know what it's all about. The way you react to me, I doubt if Randall's ever made you feel desire."

Denying that was beyond her. Her fingernails curled absently into the bear. "Nobody ever did, until that day in the gallery," she confessed.

His breath caught audibly, and his teeth ground together. "I lie awake at night, remembering how your hands felt on me," he said huskily.

She could have said the same thing to him. It would have been a perfect memory, except for what came afterward. The light went out of her eyes as she remembered Nina.

"Mine, or Nina's?" she asked dully.

He moved closer to the bed, leaning over her with one big hand resting beside her head on the thick pillow. "I'm not sleeping with Nina," he said, almost able to read the thoughts as they passed through her mind.

"Ever?" she asked cynically.

His eyes fell to her soft body and then to the bear. "I won't talk about old conquests to you, Anna," he said finally. "What happened in the past has no bearing on the present, or the future."

"Nina isn't in the past," she said, fighting not to show what his nearness was doing to her pulse. "You've made sure that everybody knew it, too, not just me."

His gaze pinned hers and he looked faintly threatening. "I've been running from you for a long time," he said shortly. "It got to be a habit, but just lately, I look at you and get so damned aroused that I can hardly function. Keeping away from you was the only thing that saved you."

Her eyebrows arched. "You're not keeping away now," she began.

"You're flat on your back in bed," he said simply. "I'm no threat to you now."

"Oh. I see," she said dully.

"You see nothing!" he raged. "My God, a blind woman…!"

"I know you want me," she burst out. "It would be hard to miss. But I want more than five feverish minutes in bed with you, Evan!"

"*Five* minutes?" he asked suggestively. "Is that how long you think it takes?"

One of her school friends had intimated as much. Actually, she didn't know how long it took, and she didn't want him to know that.

She averted her eyes. "Never mind."

He caught her chin and tilted her face up to his dark, sensuous eyes. "In five minutes I could satisfy myself," he said softly. "But I'd need another twenty to satisfy you as well."

The color came into her cheeks despite all her frantic efforts to stop it. She swallowed. "That's not fair."

He drew in a slow breath as he tried to imagine Anna in passion. He drew his thumb gently over her cheek. "No," he agreed. "It isn't. Anna…I wish you knew more about men," he added heavily. "I wouldn't have you experienced, but it would make things easier."

"You think I'll be afraid of you," she replied. "Evan, I think every woman is secretly afraid of the first time. It's like stepping into the unknown, and all the reading in the world doesn't really prepare you for it. But you've blown that natural fear up in your mind until it's completely out of proportion."

"Have I?" His eyes grew hard. "You don't know how it was for me that night," he said roughly. "You don't know what she said…!"

His anguish made her sad. She caught the big, lean hand lying beside her on the bed and drew it gently to her breast, catching her breath as she felt its warm weight. He jerked back, caught off guard, but she held his hand there, cradling it with both of hers.

"What are you doing?" he asked huskily.

"Letting you feel how frightened I am," she whispered, and pressed the heel of his hand against the furious throb of her heart.

His lips parted as he struggled to breathe normally. He looked down at his hand and began to move it, very gently, against her breast through the thin fabric of the hospital gown. The nipple went hard at once and she drew in her breath as she felt its instant response to the slow caress of his big thumb.

"You really are a big girl," he whispered sensuously.

"Do…you mind?"

"You fill my hands," he said softly. He leaned closer, his breath on her lips. "Would you like to fill my mouth, too?"

Her fingers bit into his broad shoulders. "Yes!"

He felt his body tighten, and his breath almost strangled him. His mouth brushed softly over hers, feeling its exquisite response while his hand suddenly tightened on her breast and swallowed it. His free hand went under her nape to arch her throat, and his mouth opened on hers in a kiss that was almost a statement of intent.

He tore his mouth away seconds later and stood up, visibly shuddering with frustrated desire, his face dark with it, his eyes glittering with it.

Anna stared at him hungrily, without fear, helplessly pleased at the evidence of his desire for her.

"You can see how terrified of you I am, can't you?" she whispered unsteadily. Her hands blatantly drew the gown taut around her breasts so that he could see their hard tips.

He had to swallow before he could even speak. His face was rigid as he looked at her body. "You don't understand," he said shortly. "There's more to it than this."

She moved her hands beside her head and sighed as she looked up at him. "But I'll never know, will I, because you're afraid to make love to me completely."

He laughed harshly, moving away from her to drag a cigarette out of his pocket and light it. He fumbled, because his hands were shaking so badly. "This is hardly the time or place."

"Randall wants to marry me," she lied, because she hadn't told him yet that their engagement was off. "He's not afraid to be intimate with me!"

He whirled, his eyes frightening.

She met his furious gaze evenly. "I thought it was what you wanted, to have me out of your hair for good."

"So did I," he returned curtly.

"Then you shouldn't mind if I get married and have children."

His jaw went taut. "Randall is the worst mistake you've ever made," he said. "He won't make you happy. Every time you turn around, he'll be out with some other woman."

"At least he won't be able to hurt me."

He took a long draw from the cigarette. "You don't love him. You love me."

"Isn't that just a little conceited?" she asked irritably.

"Probably, but it's true," he said quietly. He looked at her hungrily. "I don't know how I'm going to cope, Anna. But I can't let you marry Randall, feeling the way you do about me."

"You don't want ties," she countered. "You don't want marriage or children."

"How do you know?"

"Because you've said so, time and time again!" she

cried, exasperated. She lay back heavily against the pillows. "Nina's just your style. Good company and no broken heart afterward."

"She isn't," he said surprisingly. "Good company, I mean. All she wants is to go to bed with me."

"That must be a novelty."

He pursed his lips, not offended. "Not really. You want to go to bed with me, too."

She glared at him, but she didn't deny it.

He sighed wistfully and smiled at her. "You're not fragile," he said, thinking aloud. "And if I work at it, maybe I can do something about my inhibitions. God knows, I want you," he said huskily, his eyes revealing his desire. "And I'm thirty-four, plenty old enough to be thinking of settling down."

Her heart jumped. He sounded serious. "What about Nina?"

"What about her?" he asked flatly. "That's over. Finished. So is Randall," he added, his tone commanding. "You aren't going to marry him."

"Having fun arranging my life for me?" she asked breathlessly.

"Is that what I'm doing?" he mused. He finished the cigarette and put it out. He paused beside the bed and looked down at her quietly. "Tell me you don't want me, Anna."

She tried. She really did, but the words wouldn't come. She lowered her gaze.

He bent and brushed a tender kiss against her forehead. "I'll come and get you in the morning and drive you home. Polly said it was all right. She has an early-morning appointment and I volunteered."

"Evan…"

He brushed back her disheveled hair. "What?"

Her eyes were full of doubts, fears, insecurities. "Please don't play with me," she whispered. "Don't say anything you don't really mean, just because I got hurt and you feel sorry for me."

"I don't blame you for that lack of trust, little one," he replied. "Try not to brood too much. I promise you, this is no game. It isn't pity, or guilt. All right?"

She sighed. "All right."

"Good girl." He winked lazily at her. "I'll see you tomorrow."

Evan left, and as he walked out of the hospital, he seemed to relive the past few days with a vengeance. It was all catching up with him. He'd been living on nervous energy since he'd walked into the hospital with Harden. Only today was he rested enough to consider the potential consequences of what had happened to Anna, to realize how close to death she'd really come. And her last memory of him would have been painful, wounded. His eyes closed and he groaned softly. Thank God it had worked out like this. He had a second chance. Now he had to make sure he didn't blow it, even if it meant coming to grips with a lifelong fear of his own strength and size.

The next morning they wheeled her out to Evan's car in a wheelchair, and he lifted her from its confines, placing her gently in the passenger seat. It was the first time he'd ever carried her, and the sensation was odd, pleasant.

"You're terribly strong," she said breathlessly.

His jaw tautened. "I know."

He put her down and she looked into his eyes. "I like it, Evan," she whispered softly, to reassure him.

His face changed. He seemed disconcerted. He fastened her seat belt and busied himself putting her flowers and Hubert in the backseat and saying goodbye to the nurses who'd accompanied them.

They were on the way home before he spoke to Anna again. He was smoking like a furnace, something she could hardly miss.

"You never used to smoke," she remarked.

"I've been living on my nerves for several days," he replied without looking at her. "When you're back on your feet, I'll quit."

"I'm sorry you've been worried about me."

He smiled. "It isn't just worry that's done this to me, Anna," he said bluntly. "It's being near you."

She didn't know quite how to answer that, so she didn't say anything. She just stared at him, drinking in the perfection of his profile.

He glanced at her and then back at the road. "Haven't you ever wondered why I went to such lengths to avoid you? Even to the point of dragging Nina everywhere, like a shield?"

"I thought you were driving home the point that you didn't want me chasing you," she said matter-of-factly.

"Nothing quite so simple." He put out the cigarette. "I had to keep you from getting too close."

"It worked, didn't it?" she asked dully. "I got engaged to another man...."

"And I hated it," he said shortly, glaring at her. "The thought of Randall touching you the way I had made me murderous. He's damned lucky I didn't hunt him down and kill him, especially after he let you get hurt."

"He didn't..."

"If it had been me, you wouldn't have been in the car in the first place," he said shortly. "Or if you were, I wouldn't have let you out of my sight. But then, I know you better than Randall does. I would have anticipated how easily you might be tempted to leave the car."

She knew that, and it hurt. She averted her eyes to the landscape, watching it fly past the window.

"Talk about it."

She shrugged. "There isn't much to tell. He was very big and scary, and even while I was fighting him, I knew I couldn't stop him. But I thought it was me he wanted and not the jewelry."

"He might have," he said curtly. "But Randall did come along in time to prevent that, thank God."

"Yes."

"I thought you might be afraid of me at first," he said out of the blue. "The doctor said that I was apparently about the same size as the man who attacked you."

She looked at him wryly. "As if I could ever be afraid of you," she said with resignation.

He thanked God for that. He glanced at her. "About Randall…"

"We broke the engagement yesterday, Evan," she admitted finally. "He said that I'd changed since we'd been going together, and he wanted me to be happy again. He knew it wouldn't work out."

"Wise man," he said, more relieved than he could believe. "I didn't think he'd noticed the difference in you. I had," he added darkly. "But I still thought what I was doing was in your own best interest. Then you got hurt, and I realized how empty my life had been without you in it. Harden said *I'd* changed, too." He glanced at her hopeful expression. "I guess I had. Hurting you gave me no pleasure."

She stared out the window. "I'd hounded you pretty badly. I felt guilty about that."

"Hell, I loved it," he said huskily. "It was my own hangups I was fighting. When you stopped looking for me, I think I stopped living."

She smiled gently. "I'm glad."

"Yes. But we're not over the hurdles yet, little one," he said grimly. "In fact, we've hardly faced them."

"But we will," she said.

He reached over and touched her hand lightly. "Do we have a choice?" he asked heavily.

He didn't sound terribly pleased, and she worried at the strained look on his face.

"Louisa scarred you, didn't she?" she asked unexpectedly.

He hesitated. "I suppose so," he said heavily. "One of the things I vividly remember her saying is that a woman would have to be suicidal to take me on in bed." His jaw tautened as he told her. He'd never told anyone else, not even Harden.

Anna searched his rigid face. "Surely you've...been with other women?"

"With experienced women," he corrected curtly.

"But you still think you'll scare me to death?"

He stared straight ahead. "Maybe I was afraid to take the chance." He glanced at her and his eyes softened. "You're very young, Anna. You've been sheltered. More so than most women."

"That's true." She smiled gently. "But when you touch me, does it show?"

His heart beat heavily as he recalled how it had been when he put his hands on her, and his breath drew in sharply.

"It doesn't, does it, Evan?" she asked quietly, watching him. "In fact, I seemed to shock you in the gallery, when you opened your shirt and taught me how to excite you."

"For God's sake!" he groaned, and his hands gripped the steering wheel so hard that they turned white as he remembered her ardent, headlong response.

"Being innocent doesn't make me totally hopeless," she

said, as she sat back against the seat. He didn't love her, but he wanted her just short of madness. She felt reborn, whole again. She shivered inside just thinking what it would be like to seduce Evan, to lie in his arms and let him love her.

At the same time she thought of the consequences, and the smile faded. She bit her lower lip hard. She couldn't have an affair with him. Sure as the world, she'd get pregnant.

She didn't realize she'd said it aloud until the car jerked sideways and she heard Evan curse.

"What?" she asked dazedly.

"Unless you want to end up in a ditch, could you please stop talking about babies?" he asked shortly.

That could mean he wanted them, or that he didn't. She was afraid to ask which. She started talking about the weather instead, delighted that he picked up on it and began to relax with her.

She couldn't know, and he wasn't going to tell her, that the thought of a child made him go rigid with a kind of desire he'd never felt before. He hadn't allowed himself to think about children for years, because it was only Anna who made him want them. But now he wondered how she'd look with her belly swollen, her face radiant, her eyes full of dreams. He wanted her in ways she didn't realize, to come home to after a hard day's work, to talk to about his dreams and fears, to hold in the darkness when he felt alone. He wanted her so badly that his body suddenly went rigid with the force of it, and he didn't want her to see, to know how vulnerable he'd become. First he had to be sure that he could overcome his hang-ups. If he couldn't, they might not have a future.

The weather was the best diversion of all, because he

could concentrate on it and his body would relax. He focused on it all the way back to Jacobsville, refusing to allow himself to even think about Anna in maternity clothes.

# Chapter 9

Lori, the small, graying housekeeper, was waiting for them at the front door when they pulled up. Evan had forgotten the housekeeper, but he was grateful that she was in residence. He hadn't liked the idea of leaving Anna alone, and being around her tested his self-control to the limits. Only her condition kept him from going right over the edge, and it wasn't—as she thought—guilt and pity that drove him. He wanted her desperately, in every way there was.

He lifted her gently and carried her into the house, following Lori down the hall to the bedroom.

"Lord, it's so good to have you home!" she enthused, smiling at Anna. "We've all been so worried. And to have Mr. Duke home again and Miss Polly fussing over him…"

"I'm glad to be back," Anna agreed. She was trying to hide what it was doing to her to have Evan hold and carry her. She could feel the heavy thump of his heartbeat against her breasts, where they pressed into his chest, and she knew from the hardness of his face that the feel of her soft breasts was arousing him. She was shivering by the time he got into her bedroom, and grateful for Lori's presence.

"That reminds me, I've got to get to the store," Lori said suddenly.

"No!" two voices echoed.

Evan and Anna stared at each other, both faintly flushed, before they burst into laughter.

Lori stared at them. "My goodness, what was that all about?" she asked absently, frowning because her mind was already on what she needed at the store. "If you'll stay with her just a few minutes, while I run down to the supermarket, Mr. Evan?" Lori asked.

"I'll stay," he said with resignation as he laid Anna gently on the floral cover of her canopied bed.

"I'll be right back!" Lori grinned. "Anything special you want, Miss Anna?"

"Fish," Anna said. "And cheese crackers and tomato juice."

"I'll fetch them. I won't be long." She pulled the bedroom door shut, making everything much worse, and seconds later the back door closed. Then they heard Lori start Polly's car and drive off.

Evan looked down at Anna as she raised up on her elbows, her blond hair around her face in beautiful silky swirls, her blue eyes wide and soft.

He'd left his Stetson in the car. His head was bare. He was wearing a blue-printed Western shirt with jeans and boots. The shirt was taut across the muscles of his broad chest, and she watched it rise and fall with the rough unsteadiness of his breathing.

Her eyes slid farther down, to his belt and the unmistakable bulge below it. She flushed a little as her eyes slid down the powerful, muscled length of his legs and back up to his broad shoulders and darkly tanned face and glittery dark eyes.

His own gaze had gone to her legs and slowly up to the hard-nippled thrust of her breasts under the thin dress. It lingered there while his face grew visibly tauter and paler with the strain of staying where he was.

"You're aroused," he said huskily.

"So are you," she replied breathlessly.

"I haven't been any other way since you grew up," he said surprisingly. "It amazes me that you never noticed."

"I noticed that you avoided me."

He nodded.

She gnawed at her lower lip, her heart shaking her. "What happens now?" she whispered.

"We pray that Lori hurries back," he said with icy humor. "Before I do what we both want."

Her breath came out in jerky little spurts. She slowly lay back on the bed, on the floral pillow sham, her arms beside her head, her body softly trembling.

He was trembling as well, his body in anguish. But he knew all too vividly what he was going to do if he dared to touch her. They were both too aroused already to be able to stop. If he so much as kissed her, he'd take her.

"Evan," she whispered, her voice, like the soft eyes that met his, questioning. She drew up one long leg, deliberately letting the skirt fall to her upper thigh so that he could see the pale, graceful length of it.

His breathing became more audible. "Stop it."

"You want to," she whispered.

"Yes. More than you know. But it can't…happen like this," he said harshly, and deliberately turned away.

"Why?"

He leaned against the closed door, his forehead pressing there, the coolness easing the fever she'd aroused. "Because I'm desperate for you," he said huskily. "It can't be like that…the first time."

"I…wouldn't mind," she whispered, on fire to have him soothe the ache in her body.

"You would," he replied, regaining his almost-lost control. He turned, leaning his back against the door while he fumbled a cigarette into his mouth and lit it. His eyes met hers, solemnly. "Close your eyes and try to relax until it passes."

She let her eyelids fall, shivering as her taut body rippled with unknown sensations, desires, tensions.

He watched her, delighting in the knowledge that she felt exactly as he did, that her hunger could match his despite her naïveté. If Louisa's reaction to him in total intimacy hadn't scarred him so much, he wondered if he could have kept his distance from Anna.

After a minute or two, she sank into the mattress with a gentle sigh, and the tension seemed to ease from her.

"Better?" he asked quietly.

"Yes." She turned her head on the pillow and looked at him. "Is it usually like this?"

He shook his head slowly. "I've never experienced anything half as powerful in all my life."

That had to be a point in her favor. She smiled at him. After a minute he smiled back.

The door opened suddenly at his back and he moved just as Polly came in. She laughed at Evan's surprised face.

"Didn't you hear me drive up?" she asked, smiling. "How are you feeling, darling?"

Relieved, Anna almost said, because if Evan had done what her body had begged for, a very embarrassing confrontation could have ensued.

"I'm feeling tired," Anna said evasively, smiling back. "But much better. Lori ran to the store. Evan said he'd stay with me."

"Nice of you, Evan," Polly said gently.

"Yes," he replied evenly. "If you're going to be home for a while, I need to get some work done." He smiled at Anna. "I've let things go lately."

"I wonder why?" Polly mused. "Thank you for bringing her home," she added seriously.

"No problem." He glanced at Anna, trying not to show how much he hated leaving her, even for a day. "I promised to help Harden shift some cattle this afternoon, but I'll be back tomorrow. I've got some videos you might like to watch."

She managed a smile. "That would be nice."

"Yes, it would," Polly said. "Duke wanted to take me out tomorrow, but I hesitated, because I hated leaving Anna alone. We're going fishing," she added. "Duke and I want to talk."

Anna brightened. "Really?"

"Don't get your hopes up too high," Polly said. "But cross your fingers."

"I'll do that little thing," she promised.

"And I'll babysit," Evan said with a mocking smile.

Anna had to fight not to blush at the images he was conjuring up with that sensuous tone, but she reminded herself that she mustn't read too much into his innuendoes. He wanted her. Maybe it had blinded him to reality.

"Then I'll buy those new jeans I saw today." Polly grinned. "Evan, you're sure you don't mind?"

He looked at Anna and had to fight down another wave of throbbing heat. "No," he said huskily. "I don't mind."

Anna wanted to beg him to stay, because her scruples were beginning to give under the weight of her desire. But when he came tomorrow, he might lie beside her while they watched television, and with no one in the house—since tomorrow was Lori's day off—anything might happen. She knew she could never say no to Evan if he really wanted her. But giving in to him would be a big mistake, she realized sadly as reality punctured her bright dreams. His sense of honor might even force him into marriage if he compromised her. She didn't want a reluctant bridegroom. Love on one side would never be enough.

Evan smiled, but he didn't look at her again. He left, and Polly went back to her daydreams, unaware of Anna's rising fears.

That night she got up long enough to have supper with her parents, enjoying the way they talked to each other and to her. She felt part of a family for the first time in years. And Polly was actually radiant.

Later she excused herself and went to lie down, leaving Duke and Polly alone together. When she fell asleep after hours of daydreaming about the day ahead and Evan, they were still sitting in the living room talking.

Evan arrived late the next morning with two newly released movies in his hand, looking rakish and barely awake in denim and a checked Western shirt. He also looked half out of humor.

"I was up late doing book work," he explained to Polly, forcing a smile. In fact, he'd lain awake worrying about what he was going to do if he lost control with Anna and scared her half to death. He knew his fears were irrational, but he'd lived with them far too long to be able to dismiss them now.

Duke had stayed the night at the house, but he was dressed and ready to leave before Polly awoke and got dressed herself. Lori had served breakfast and gone out with friends to see a movie.

"How's my girl?" Duke asked Anna as he joined his wife and daughter and Evan in Anna's bedroom where she lay, dressed in a long red skirt and a red-and-gold patterned blouse, stretched out on top of her covers with her long blond hair soft around her face and her pretty feet bare.

Anna kissed his tan cheek when he bent down. "Doing fine. I hope you and Mom catch a lot of fish."

"I'll settle for one pretty one," Duke murmured dryly, and Polly actually blushed.

Anna smiled at them. "Go away and enjoy yourselves."

They exchanged glances, but they didn't argue.

"Don't worry about her," Evan told them solemnly. "I'll take good care of her."

He was saying more than the words implied, and they knew it. Polly saw Duke relax visibly, and after a brief conversation, they left.

Evan walked them out and then returned to Anna's room, pausing in the doorway to look at her. She looked delicious. His heart began to run wild, just at the sight of her.

"Do you feel like watching these?" he asked, holding up two tapes of just-released movies.

"Yes," she said huskily, thinking how sweet it would be if he lay down with her on the bed and let her lie against him. Her face flamed with desire.

He had to turn away from that expression. He was glad the housekeeper was around. If she hadn't been, he wasn't sure he could manage to keep his hands off Anna.

"Lori's here, isn't she?" he asked tautly, to make sure, while he loaded the first movie into the VCR and turned on the television before he started it.

"Well…no," she said. "It's her day off."

His jaw tautened. He actually shivered.

"Will it help if I promise not to seduce you?" she asked with a lightness she didn't feel. Her heart was racing.

He felt his body tauten as he looked at her across the room, his eyes falling helplessly to her blouse. "You wouldn't have to, don't you know?" he asked on a harsh laugh. "All you have to do is touch me."

Her heart ran wild. The truth of it was in his face, and all her dreams seemed to come true at once. She held out her arms to him, burning up with need.

He groaned, but he couldn't help himself. He went to her, feeling her cold hands curve around his neck as he bent, easing her back on the bed. It was wrong, he shouldn't. But her body was yielding and soft and exquisitely formed, and he felt himself going rigid long before his mouth lowered to her parted lips.

His body went down alongside hers on the mattress, his mouth fitting over hers with warm, slow mastery as they sank back onto the quilted coverlet.

It was heaven. Anna nibbled eagerly at his lips, loving the taste of him, the warmth and strength of his body against hers. But just as he deepened the kiss and his arms tightened, she gasped, and he drew back instantly.

"Did I hurt you?" he asked curtly, his eyes worried. "My God, sometimes I hate my own size!"

"You didn't hurt me," she said and lowered her eyes to his hard mouth. "I go hot all over when you kiss me like that," she whispered huskily.

He relaxed. His fingers traced her cheek. "All that worry, wasted," he mused with forced lightness.

"Do you really think I could ever be afraid of you, Evan?" she asked unsteadily. "Don't you know already that you could do anything to me and I'd let you?"

His eyes flashed. He bent hungrily to her lips as one big arm slid under her and lifted her against him. His mouth caressed and withdrew, brushed and lifted, as he aroused her with maddening skill until she was clinging and following his lips with her own, trying to make him end the torment.

"What do you want?" he whispered.

"Kiss me!" she moaned.

His teeth nibbled lazily at her lower lip. "Isn't that what I'm doing?"

"Do it right. Open your mouth and do it...!"

He did, at the same time shifting his big body so that his hips were squarely over hers, his arousal hot and blatant as it rested on her soft belly.

She gasped at the intimacy.

He lifted his mouth from hers and looked into her shocked eyes. He didn't move for a long moment, but that wasn't fear in her eyes. He moved softly and she grimaced.

He realized then that it was embarrassment, not distaste, and he smiled gently as he levered his body to one side. She smiled back, her face coloring delicately.

He eased one powerful leg between both of hers and she stiffened.

He shook his head. "No. This is part of lovemaking. I want you to know everything there is to know about my body. You have to, before we go any further."

She had to fight her own shyness, but after a minute she relented and let him rest against her.

"Don't be afraid," he said, his voice deep and sensual. "I'm letting you learn me, that's all."

She relaxed even more, and as the shock of intimacy slowly wore off, she began to enjoy the feel of his body.

He knew that she had no experience by which to judge him. That relaxed him a little. There was so much that she didn't know, but at least, thank God, there was no apprehension in her face. He'd never been able to make Louisa lie with him like this at all. In fact, she'd found intimacy with him almost distasteful. He still remembered how she cringed when he touched her breasts, and she'd never liked his mouth on them.

He drew his fingers slowly over Anna's breasts, the sound of flesh against fabric loud in the tense silence as he gently teased around the nipple that suddenly became taut. He held her eyes the whole time, heard her breathing change even as she allowed him the caress with damning generosity.

She gasped and arched toward his hand, trying to make him end the torment as he touched everywhere except against the hardness that ached for him.

"Gently," he whispered. "I'm going to do what you want me to, but let me make you burn for it first."

She colored, but she didn't protest his touch. She lay back against the pillows, her face flushed, waiting, trembling, as he built the torment almost to anguish and she moaned.

His big hand tensed under her, and he leaned closer, his dark eyes filling the world. "Is it bad?" he whispered.

"Yes!" Her nails bit into his shoulders as she let him see the helpless reaction of his body to his caress. "Evan, please! Oh, please!"

He drew his nose softly against hers, his breath on her cheek, her lips, and still his knuckles brushed with maddening slowness just at the very edge of her taut nipple.

Then, very gently, he caught the hard nub in his fingertips. She felt a rush of heat in her belly, and a long shudder rippled through her. She could barely see him through a blur of anguished desire, her expression one of taut abandon as she arched upward and gasped at the unbelievable pleasure.

Evan watched her with indulgent tenderness. "So hungry," he whispered. "I could almost satisfy you just by putting my mouth on you, couldn't I, little one?"

The intimacy of the statement made her flush, but she didn't protest when he began to flick open the buttons of her blouse with careless deftness.

"Lie still," he said when she touched his wrist in a faint protest. "Let me look at you."

"I've never," she began shakily, her eyes enormous.

"My God, don't you think I know?" he asked huskily. His eyes flashed as he pulled the blouse gently aside and then snapped the front catch of the bra. He drew it away from her swollen breasts and caught his breath at the beauty of her creamy body with its mauve nipples.

"I'm so...big," she whispered, almost apologetic.

"You're as self-conscious about your size as I am about mine," he said quietly. He touched her, as lightly as a breath, watching her face as she gave herself up to his hands. "You please me," he said, his voice deep and exquisitely tender. "You arouse me as no other woman ever has, ever will. You're delicious, Anna," he breathed, bending toward her breasts with unbearable slowness. "I want to eat you up..."

His mouth settled over the hard-tipped mound and began to pull at it, nibble at it, with tender absorption. Anna cried out. The pleasure she experienced was so overwhelming that tears stung her eyes. She clung to him, her shaking hands grasping his thick hair, pulling him closer, closer...!

One big hand was under her skirt. Dimly she registered

its progress, felt his touch on her slender legs and then on her flat belly.

"Anything," she gasped at his ear. "Anything you want… Evan!"

His hand contracted on her soft flesh and just for an instant, he gave in to the need that was consuming him. His mouth grew rough, like his insistent hands, and Anna yielded completely. His strength delighted her, his ardor made her weak all over. She bit his shoulder in her own oblivion, hard.

He caught his breath and jerked up, his face unfamiliar in passion.

"I…I'm sorry," she faltered, embarrassed at the expression in his eyes. "I bit you."

"Yes." There was something unfamiliar in the way he was looking at her, in the set rigidity of his face. His eyes fell to her body, to the faint redness where his hungry mouth had touched it. He actually shuddered.

"I thought you'd be afraid of me like this," he said quietly.

"Why?" she whispered.

"I could hurt you," he ground out. He grimaced at the marks he'd left on her breast. He touched it softly. "I didn't mean to lose my head like this!"

That she could make him lose it gave her a sense of wild elation. "It doesn't hurt, you know," she said with a gentle smile. "In fact, I liked it."

"Dangerous, to say that to me," he said huskily.

"I'm not antique glass, Evan. I won't break if you're a little rough with me."

She moved closer to him, her eyes searching his as she slid her leg gently against his and laid her hand flat against his shirt.

"What do you want?" he asked softly, delighted and overwhelmed by her desire for him.

"Can I touch you, here?" she whispered.

He hesitated for only a minute before he gave in to the need for her hands on him. He snapped open the pearly buttons and tugged the shirttail out of his jeans, holding her eyes while he threw the shirt onto the floor.

She rested her forehead against the broad, hair-roughened expanse of muscle and her hands caught in the hair, tugging it sensuously. "Like this?" she whispered, wanting nothing more than to please him. "Isn't this what you like?"

"Yes," he said in a choked tone. His hands slid into her hair, moving her forehead against him. "Kiss me the way I kissed you. Here," he emphasized, guiding her mouth to one side of his chest.

She caught her breath. It had never occurred to her that men had nipples or could be aroused by having them touched. The possibilities made her dizzy. She slid her lips through the thick hair until she found the hard thrust of a flat male nipple. She nuzzled it first with her nose, then with her lips, then with her teeth. Evan's big body went rigid and shuddered when she took the nipple in her teeth. She loved the way he responded to her. Her mouth nuzzled all over his chest as he eased onto his back to give her the total freedom of his body. His eyes closed, his chest rippled as she touched it. Her lips pulled softly at the other nipple and he actually groaned. Amazing, she thought, delicious, to be able to make him even momentarily at the mercy of his need for her. She drew her lips daringly down to the wide belt at his hips and bit him delicately just below his navel.

He shuddered and arched, crying out. Anna lifted her head, shocked and a little frightened by his reaction to so gentle a caress.

She didn't recognize him when she saw his face. His eyes were tormented, his face dark with passion, his mouth a thin line.

"I'm sorry," she said quickly. "Evan, I'm sorry, did I hurt you?"

"For God's…sake…Anna!"

He whipped her over beside him, pausing just long enough to strip the open blouse and bra from her, throwing them carelessly on the floor, and then he arched above her and looked down, his big body shivering with need.

Her breasts were big; full and firm with dark mauve tips that quickly grew hard as he looked at them.

Instinctively her arm moved to cover herself, but he caught it and pulled her up into a sitting position.

"No," he said gruffly. "You belong to me. Let me look."

After a minute, she gave in and sat trembling, flushing as he stared at her breasts. This kind of intimacy was new, and a little scary.

"Only you," she whispered unsteadily.

"Only me," he said, his voice deep and slow and husky. His eyes darkened. "God, you're beautiful, Anna," he said roughly. "Absolutely beautiful!"

She seemed to blossom at the words, her back arching unconsciously. "Evan," she whispered, shivering. "Evan, I'll die if you don't touch me…!"

He felt the same way. He reached for her hungrily. "So much for patience," he managed. His jaw clenched as he held her upper arms tightly and let his eyes feed on her beauty. "This is where we could get in over our heads very quickly," he said through his teeth, and he brought her breasts suddenly against the thick rasping mat of hair that covered him from throat to stomach. "I don't even know if I can stop," he bit off against her mouth as he took it hungrily.

Anna stiffened and shivered at the contact of her taut breasts with his bare chest, the most intimate she'd ever experienced. Evan held her by the rib cage and slowly, torturously began to drag her breasts against that thicket of hair with sensuous movements that were like setting a match to dry wood.

She hadn't known that her body could shudder with ecstasy from just the feel of a man's hairy chest against her bare breasts. But her nails bit into Evan's big shoulders and she moved with him, her body shivering as the delicious contact aroused her to fever pitch.

"Do it…hard," she whispered hoarsely, her eyes closed as she swayed against him. "Rub me against you…very hard!"

He wasn't even thinking now. His body was reacting predictably to the ardor she aroused in him. He looked where they touched, watching her hard nipples drag against his warm chest, feeling them like brands on his body. He bent her across him and increased the ardent pressure, moving her from side to side now, hearing her shaky moans, feeling the bruising bite of her fingernails. She sobbed and her mouth pressed hard against his bare shoulders. She bit him again, quite hard, her tongue drawing circles on his skin in helpless passion.

One of his hands had slid to her lower spine and was grinding her rhythmically into the taut heat of him while his mouth suddenly bent to hers and possessed it fiercely.

At that moment, she would have let him do anything he liked to her. When his mouth lifted, she let her body arch backward, her firm breasts jutting toward his lips, her eyes closed as she yielded her body to him completely.

The action made Evan shiver. He knew what she was saying, without words. She would give him anything he wanted, do anything he asked of her. He could lay her down on the bed and strip her and make her his, and she would allow him to.

That submission stopped him, when nothing else would have. He lifted his head slowly, his eyes focusing hungrily on her breasts. He was faintly aware of the stab of her nails into his shoulders, but it was her flushed, hungry face that caught his attention. He'd never seen her look more beautiful.

He eased her cheek against the reckless throb of his bare chest and gently held her there, fighting for sanity.

She rubbed her breasts against him helplessly, her lips pressing soft kisses against his throat.

"Don't," he whispered, stilling her. "The feel of you is driving me out of my mind."

"I know." She nibbled at his chin. "We could make love," she whispered unsteadily. "Right here."

His big hands firmed on her shoulders. "No."

"You want me," she said.

"Viciously," he agreed. "But we can't make love on your bed in the middle of the day, when Lori or your parents could come home unexpectedly and find us."

"We could lock the doors," she moaned.

He lifted his head and tilted her chin up to his. "Take deep breaths," he said quietly. "Let yourself relax. I'm not going to use you like a woman I've bought for the night, Anna. Cheap sex isn't what I'm after, despite the fact that our lovemaking got a little out of hand just now."

She let her eyes fall to his bare chest. "A little?" she whispered on a nervous laugh.

"I told you how it would be," he reminded her. He held her eyes and slid one big hand up her body to cup and caress her firm breasts. "You really are a big girl," he whispered, smiling gently. "Just my size."

She blushed, but she smiled, too, arching so that his hand moved to encompass her even more fully.

"Like it?" he asked huskily.

"Don't you know?" she countered.

He bent his head and the hand at her back moved her so that he could put his mouth over the breast he was cupping. He suckled at it gently, nibbled, caressed, bit, until she curled into him with a helpless moan. She loved the moist heat of his mouth on her skin, remembering the first time he'd ever done it with a layer of fabric in the way.

She held him when he started to lift his head. "Just…a little more, please," she whimpered. "Bite…me…!"

And he'd been afraid of frightening her, he thought ironically as he gave in to her pleas. He laid her back on the bed and fed on her breasts like a starving man, delighting in her cries of pleasure, the clasp of her arms, the trembling vulnerability of her yielded body.

His mouth slid back up to her open lips and without thinking of the consequences, his body slowly levered over her, one powerful leg insinuating itself between hers so that he could bring them into total intimacy.

She caught her breath and clutched at him, shivering. He lifted his head then and looked into her wide eyes.

"It will probably hurt like hell," he said flatly, one lean hand going under her to press her hips up into his. "Especially if you've never even played at intimacy before."

"I haven't. But if it isn't you," she whispered, "it won't be anybody, ever. I love you!"

He groaned and his eyes closed. She made all his fears seem groundless. She loved him. He began to wonder if Louisa ever had, or if she'd only wanted him for his position, his wealth. Anna had insinuated as much, as Harden had years ago, and now he had to face the fact that it might have been true.

He brushed his mouth gently over her bare shoulders, her throat, her lips. "I'll be rough with you," he said in something like anguish. "I won't be able to help it, don't you understand? I lose control so easily with you. Oh, God, I've probably left bruises on you already…!"

She kissed him softly, rubbing her nose lovingly against his. "You haven't seen your shoulder yet, have you?" she asked tenderly, and smiled.

He laughed softly. "Yes. You bit me, didn't you?"

"Very hard," she whispered shakily. "I didn't know it was going to feel like that, or that you'd do what you did to me." She dug her fingers into the thick hair that covered his chest. "I thought I might faint when you started rubbing your chest against me."

"There are times when I'm not sorry about this thicket," he admitted against her lips. "You were very, very aroused."

"I still am," she said softly. "I wish we could make love."

"So do I. But we can't, like this."

"You could undress," she suggested half-humorously.

"You don't understand." He moved to her side and stretched a little jerkily, pulling her down against him with her cheek pillowed on his chest. "What we're doing is something that belongs in the confines of marriage." He searched her eyes quietly while his fingers gentled on her breast. "If I give you a baby, it's going to be after we're married, not before."

She didn't think she could have heard him properly. "You don't want to get married," she faltered.

"Oh, but I do," he said doggedly. He lowered his mouth to hers and kissed it slowly, hotly. "I'll take the chance, if you will. Say yes, Anna," he breathed.

"Yes!" The word burst from her like a rainbow of sound and Evan took a long breath and damned the consequences.

"No long engagement, either," he whispered. "We'll get the license tomorrow."

"So soon?" she gasped.

"I can't bear to be away from you for five minutes lately," he said, his eyes glittering with barely leashed passion. "I want you with me all the time, day and night. I want you under me in bed, Anna," he whispered sensually, nibbling her lower lip while he played with her lips and stroked her breast. "I want your naked body writhing under the hardness of mine…!"

She met his mouth halfway, her body turning, accepting the crush of his, begging for more. It was all he could do to get away from her. He rolled away and got to his feet, keeping his back to her until he could stop shuddering. He reached for a cigarette, but they were in the shirt he didn't remember discarding. He reached down and retrieved it from the floor, along with her blouse and bra.

Anna was sitting up, breathing raggedly, and his eyes went pointedly to the thrust of her pretty breasts.

"Exquisite," he whispered breathlessly. "I could look at you like that for the rest of my life. But in the interests of your chastity, I think you'd better cover them up. Quick."

He tossed her garments to her, watching her flush and jerk trying to get them back on again.

The droll humor soothed her embarrassment. She was a little shy of him now. He seemed to sense it, because he pulled her up from the bed and held her gently. "You still don't know exactly what you could be letting yourself in for. I was in control most of the time today. But when I lose control, and eventually I will, you might not like what happens."

"I'm still trying to figure out what it is that I'm supposed to be so afraid of."

"I'm oversize," he said quietly. "I've always had to pull my punches, ever since I was a boy. Even now…" He broke off. "I keep remembering Louisa," he admitted finally, and he winced.

This, she thought, was going to take time and patience. But if she was careful, maybe she could heal those scars. "I'm not fragile," she said, her voice soft and hesitant. "I want you as much as you want me. And I love you."

His hand touched her lips with exquisite tenderness. "You make all my worst fears sound ridiculous."

"They are," she replied. She closed her eyes while he kissed her with something like reverence. "Are you going to stay with me?"

He laughed softly. "How can I stay away?" he countered. "There aren't that many women in Jacobsville who worship the ground I walk on."

She glared at him. "Go ahead, rub it in."

"I wasn't. I feel pretty arrogant and smug right now, if you want to know." He nibbled at her mouth. "Now let's sit down, in the living room," he emphasized, "and watch some movies, before we end up in bed again."

"We will, eventually," she said doggedly.

He sighed. "Eventually," he agreed. "First I have to work up the nerve," he said under his breath. He brushed a careless kiss against her forehead and, minutes later, started the VCR in the living room. Evan settled her in the curve of his arm and wondered quietly how he was going to go on living if she ever turned away from him out of fear.

## Chapter 10

Evan wasn't wasting much time arranging the wedding, Anna discovered the next morning, when he came to pick her up to apply for the license. They'd told Polly and Duke the day before and decided to wait overnight before they started the paperwork, but nobody was surprised by the news. The other couple only grinned.

Anna was as close to heaven as she'd been in her life. Evan was openly affectionate now, kissing her when he came into the house, wrapping her up against him when they walked. If he didn't care about her, he was certainly a good actor.

After they applied for the license and had a blood test, Evan took her out to lunch at a restaurant downtown.

"You aren't eating much," he observed when she barely touched her roast beef.

She looked up at him, her eyes soft and loving. "I'm still in shock," she confessed. "I can hardly believe it, even now."

His dark eyes slid over her face possessively. "I'd never thought about marriage before," he confessed. "Not seriously, at least, even if I did lip service to the idea of wanting a home and a family."

"You used to say that they all trampled you trying to get to Harden," she recalled with a smile.

His big shoulders rose and fell. "In a way, it was true. Harden hated women, so naturally they all loved him. Especially Miranda, fortunately for him," he added with a grin.

"I used to think that if Harden could get married, anybody could," she admitted. "He was a real woman hater."

"No less than Connal, until Pepi came up on his blind side," he agreed. He caught her hand in his and turned it over, stroking her ring finger absently. "I haven't even bought you a ring," he remarked.

The license and the blood test had convinced her that he was serious, but the mention of a ring made her heart beat faster. That was commitment.

She looked up into his eyes with pure joy.

"Do you want a diamond, Anna?" he asked gently.

"I'm not sure…"

"Don't, for God's sake, tell me you want an emerald," he said, his dark eyes flashing. "I won't buy you one."

He sounded viciously jealous of the emerald Randall had given her. She had to hide a smile. "No, I don't want an emerald," she admitted. "I don't suppose colored stones are a very good investment, are they?"

He scowled. "Honey, I'm not buying it for an investment," he said gently. "This isn't a business deal."

"I'm sorry." She couldn't very well tell him that she didn't understand why he was marrying her. She was sure that he cared, a little. It was just that she wanted him to be in love, as she was. He was attentive and kind and even affectionate, but she wasn't sure of him.

What she didn't know was that he hadn't abandoned his fears. He was going ahead with the wedding despite them, mostly out of worry that she might go back to Randall. He was taking a terrible chance on her age and innocence, despite her confession of undying love.

She sensed his reservations. Nina still bothered her. That old flame had turned into a raging fire just before Anna was attacked. How could she be sure that Evan didn't feel something for Nina? How could she be sure that he wasn't marrying her out of pity and guilt and helpless desire?

She sipped her coffee absently, her eyes avoiding his.

In answer to all her unspoken worries, Nina walked in the door of the restaurant, alone, and spotted Evan.

He saw the woman coming and cursed viciously to himself. His manners outweighed his anger, so he pushed back his chair and stood up, but his eyes weren't welcoming.

"Well, hello," Nina gushed. She went up to Evan and blatantly kissed him, despite his obvious reticence. "How are you, darling? I haven't seen you for ages! What have you been doing?"

"Getting engaged," he said flatly. "Anna and I are going to be married."

Nina actually froze. She didn't move or speak for a long moment, and then she laughed harshly. "You're marrying Anna? After all the time you spent running from her? Well, well, what did you do, Evan, get her pregnant?"

"That's enough," Evan said coldly.

Nina stared at Anna with pure hatred in her eyes. "You aren't stupid enough to think he loves you? All he's capable of is wanting! I should know!" She was almost shaking with rage, and attracting the attention of half a dozen other diners as well. "I gave him everything I had, and I couldn't hold him!"

"Nina, stop it," Evan said quietly. "You're making a spectacle of yourself."

Her lower lip trembled as she stared at him. Despite her embarrassment, Anna felt a terrible sympathy for her. Nina had been in love with Evan. It was painfully obvious.

"Just my luck…to be the wrong kind of woman to get you to the altar," Nina sobbed at Evan. "Everybody said experience appealed to you, but it wasn't true, was it? You're robbing the cradle at that…!"

She whirled suddenly and ran out of the restaurant, still crying.

Evan sat back down heavily. "I'm sorry about that," he told Anna, his voice strained but tender.

"She loved you," Anna said softly.

"Yes," he agreed. "But I didn't love her. You can't force yourself to care about somebody, Anna. That's life."

She knew that. She looked at Evan with horror. She was marrying him, and he didn't love her any more than he loved Nina. What kind of relationship could they build on a one-sided attraction? Eventually even desire would wane, and what would be left?

Evan cursed roundly when he got a good look at her face. He helped her up and went to pay the check, ignoring the curious stares of the other patrons. Nina had destroyed Anna's radiant mood, and his own. He'd thought the woman realized when he didn't call that he was no longer interested. It was his own fault. He'd used her to keep Anna at bay and she'd misunderstood his continuing attention. He should have had a long talk with her, but Anna's situation had claimed all his faculties.

He escorted Anna back to the car, his whole demeanor quiet and preoccupied.

"I think we'll wait and get the rings in the morning, if you don't mind," he told her when he pulled up in front of her house. "I have some things to take care of."

"It's all right with me," Anna replied. "The day's been rather spoiled anyway."

He cut off the engine and turned toward her. He winced at her bleak expression. "I'm sorry," he said huskily.

"You can't help it that women fall all over themselves trying to get to you." She laughed bitterly. "After all, I'm one of them, aren't I?"

"No," he said flatly. "You're not one in a crowd. I've asked you to marry me, Anna, not to spend a few feverish hours in bed with me!"

"I do realize what a great honor you're doing me." She looked at him with something approximating panic. "What kind of life will we have, falling all over your discarded lovers every time we go out to eat? Evan, I don't want this," she said wildly. "I can't marry you…!"

His hand shot out and caught her arm, dragging her over against him so that her head fell back against his shoulder.

"No, you don't," he said huskily. "You're not backing out."

"Yes, I—!"

He stopped the frantic words with his mouth. She fought him, but only for a few seconds. The heat and mastery of his mouth slowly began to weaken her struggles. She couldn't resist him. Her lips parted and her arms went up and around his neck, as she gave him back the long, slow kiss. Her pulses began to throb with the sweetness of being in his arms.

"You aren't playing fair," she whispered, shaken, when he finally lifted his head.

"I'm not playing, period," he replied, his dark eyes piercing, steady on hers. "Nina knew the score from the very beginning. I made no promises, ever."

"You used her," she whispered miserably.

His face tautened. "Yes," he admitted curtly. "I did. At the time, I thought I was protecting you. I used her shamefully. She had every right to be upset about that, but she can't pretend that she didn't know what I was doing. She was willing."

Her lower lip trembled. "You slept with her!" she accused huskily.

"Years ago, if you have to know," he replied flatly. "Not since. Certainly not since she's been back in town. I told you before, I can't even get aroused by other women, least of all Nina!"

Her breasts rose and fell in a slow, heavy sigh. She let her cheek rest against him. She stared past him out the window. It was misting rain and cloudy. Like her life, she thought.

"Why do you want to marry me, Evan?" she asked finally.

He lifted his head, scowling. "What?"

"Why do you want to marry me?" she repeated. "Is it pity, or guilt, or desire, or a little of all three?"

"My God, you still don't trust me, do you?" he asked. He sounded almost defeated. "I can't blame you, but if you have so little faith in my motives, why are you willing to go through with it?"

She looked up at him. "Because I love you," she said simply.

He touched her loosened, disheveled hair. "You aren't sure of me," he replied. "If you loved me, wouldn't you be?"

Her eyes grew sad. "Not really. It's hard to be sure of someone when you don't know how they feel."

He let his eyes fall to her mouth. "How do you think I feel?" he hedged.

"I don't know. You've been very different since the accident," she replied. "Before, you made it clear how you felt about me, that you wanted me out of your life. Then I got hurt and all at once, you were willing to marry me."

"You make me sound fickle, Anna," he said, but he couldn't deny the truth of what she was insinuating.

"Not fickle. Just uncertain. You can't blame me for feeling the same way. You've never really told me what you felt."

And he couldn't. Not just yet. He still had too many misgivings, too many fears.

He touched her mouth lightly with his forefinger. "Will words convince you?" he asked quietly. "Somehow, I don't think so. You've got it fixed in your mind that I'm only sorry for you. Nothing I say is going to change that. You're just going to have to wait and see."

Fear flickered under her eyelashes. "You'd be tied to me, don't you see?" she asked gently. "You'd hate it!"

His mouth covered hers. He lifted her into a warmer, closer embrace, his lips driving every worry out of her mind. His hand slid inside her blouse, under the bra, with blatant mastery. She felt his fingers against her soft, bare flesh. She stiffened and gasped at the surge of pleasure it gave her.

His teeth caught at her lower lip, gently teasing it. "We're going to have the most unusual wedding night in history," he said with black humor. "It will probably be the first time that the groom has jitters."

She drew back a little. "Are you afraid to make love to me?" she asked hesitantly.

"Isn't it obvious?" he asked darkly. "My God, I've fought

this. And in the end, I couldn't give you up, not even for your own good."

"Evan, it's not going to be that bad," she said, trying to reassure him. He looked…she couldn't quite decide how he looked. "I can see the doctor before we're married. If he thinks there's going to be any, well, any difficulty, he can take care of it for me."

His jaw tautened. "Your virginity isn't what concerns me."

"Then what?"

He drew in a rough breath and looked down at the bulge of his hand under her blouse. Absently his fingers caressed her, loving the softness of her skin. "Anna, I could hurt you so badly," he said huskily. "It might bring back terrible memories of the night you were attacked. And quite frankly, past a certain point, a man can't stop."

She reached up and nibbled at his mouth. "Then you'll have to make me crazy first, won't you?" she whispered. "Like you did…yesterday when you opened your shirt and held me against you…Evan!"

His mouth bit into hers. She arched closer, her fingers pressing his intruding hand to her breast. For a few seconds, he actually seemed blind and deaf, his mouth devouring and sweet.

He groaned and pulled her across his lap, turning her so that her belly pressed against his hardness. He ground her into him, feeling her tremble.

"Yes," she whispered into his mouth. She moved deliberately, loving the feel of him, the raging arousal that she seemed to kindle in him so effortlessly.

His hand tangled painfully in her hair as his tongue drove into the softness of her mouth. His free hand, at the base of her spine, rocked her rhythmically against him, sending ripples of pure ecstasy through his rigid body.

He felt her soft trembling with wonder, felt her submission. His fingers went to her blouse and began to unfasten it. Thank God the yard was deserted and Polly's car was gone. They were totally alone.

He lifted his head long enough to get the blouse out of his way and unclasp her bra.

"Yes," she murmured. She sat up, impatiently helping him rid her of the unwanted fabric. But then her hands went to his own shirt and unfastened the pearly snaps.

"Anna…" he began, fighting for control.

"I want to feel you against me," she whispered hungrily. She linked her arms around his neck and brushed the tips of her breasts against his hair-roughened chest.

"Anna!" he groaned harshly.

She saw his face contort and recognized the rigid mask of pleasure.

"Is this how to do it?" she whispered, moving her torso even harder against his. "Teach me, Evan. Show me how to make love."

"My…God, you don't…need lessons!" he managed.

"Here," she said, tugging at his head as she arched back against his arm, her eyes half-closed. "Do…what you did to me yesterday. Do it hard!"

He was out of his mind. He barely realized it as his mouth settled helplessly on one dusky hard-tipped breast. He suckled at it, feeling her body ripple with pleasure as he fed on her softness. His fingers cupped her, caressed her while he discovered the hard tip with his tongue, his lips. And she lay there and let him, vibrating with pleasure, her soft sighs lost in the rough groans that burst from his mouth.

"Evan, it feels so good," she moaned feverishly. Her hands tangled in his thick hair, holding him to her hungry body. "It feels so good, so good!"

"You taste of rose petals." He lifted his head and looked at her, at the soft flesh with its deep flush that his mouth had caused. He took a slow breath and let his hand slowly caress her. "I want you."

"I want you, too." Her back arched gently, her eyes glazed with desire. "Can't we…go somewhere and be alone?"

His jaw tautened. "Risky," he managed.

"I don't care. I want you to look at me," she said dizzily. "I want to look at you!"

He wanted to scream. He had to think. He had to protect her. She arched her back again and rubbed her breasts slowly against him.

"All right," he said shakily.

He made her sit up, helping her into the blouse again. He started the car without a word. He didn't dare look at her or he'd wreck it.

He drove quietly, and quickly, to the Tremayne lake. It was deserted during the week, and no one ever went there. He stopped the car, turned off the ignition, and got out.

Anna lifted her arms as he bent to carry her down to the grassy bank of the lake.

"This is insane," he whispered as he laid her down in the grass and went down beside her. "We'll go too far."

"It's all right," she said softly. She pulled off her blouse and let him look at her, totally without inhibitions. He was going to marry her. She loved him. Now she had to convince him that she wasn't frightened of him.

Evan could hardly breathe for the pounding of his heart as he stared at her soft, swollen breasts.

"You're a virgin," he groaned.

"Would you rather I let Randall see me like this?" she whispered.

His eyes flashed. "No. I would not." He stripped off his

shirt and his belt before he laid her back on the grass and spread his broad, dark chest over her breasts. He held her eyes as he began to move his torso sensually over hers, letting his hair-roughened muscles drag arousingly over the hard tips of her breasts.

Her nails dug into his powerful upper arms as the motion kindled a sudden, shocking desire. She gasped jerkily.

"And this is only the beginning, Anna," he said roughly. "It gets worse. Much worse."

He bent to her mouth. He'd never kissed her like this, in such a deliberately arousing way. He teased and tormented her soft mouth until she was openly begging for his, driven half mad by the sensual movements of his body against her bare breasts.

She was almost in tears by the time he finally relented, and his tongue penetrated her mouth in one deep, smooth motion. She was so aroused that she actually cried out and went rigid, pulsating with feverish need as the kiss she thought would satisfy her only aroused a deeper hunger.

Her legs moved against Evan's helplessly. He felt her anguished need and his big body levered over hers. He eased her legs apart and slid slowly between them.

He lifted his dark head. His eyes were black with arousal, his swollen lips parted on jerky breaths. He rested his weight on his forearms and held her dazed, hungry eyes while he deliberately pushed down.

She felt him in an intimacy that she'd never shared with anyone before. Her eyes dilated and her lips parted on a gasp as she felt the full force of his desire.

He watched her, certain that it was going to be just as it had been with Louisa. She was going to run…

Even as he thought it, her long legs began to tangle shyly with his. Her hips lifted, very gently. He stiffened and shuddered, even though his eyes never left hers.

She did it again, her face radiant as she watched his helpless reaction.

"This is very, very dangerous," he bit off. "If you arouse me enough, I won't be able to stop."

"I don't mind."

His big hand caught her thigh and stilled her under him. "You don't understand. I could make you pregnant."

She smiled gently. "You don't understand," she replied. "I want a baby with you."

He actually shuddered. For one mad instant, he looked into her eyes and gave in to her. His hand moved from her thigh to the base of her spine and he pushed her legs farther apart as he settled completely between them in a blatant urgency that made her moan sharply.

"This is what you're inviting," he said roughly, and pushed, hard. "It will hurt like hell if I'm this aroused when it happens!"

That was when she first began to make sense of all the warnings, all the misgivings. She relaxed under his weight and her eyes held his fierce black ones.

"Oh," she whispered.

He was trembling. "Seen the light, have you?" he choked. "I hope to God you haven't seen it too late. Lie still!" he bit off, anchoring her with a merciless hand. He looked at her, shivering with reaction as he fought to control himself.

She watched him, shaken by his vulnerability, by her own ability to affect him. Sex had been a vaguely frightening mystery, but now it was a wonderous surprise. She had a pretty good idea of what it entailed and exactly why Evan was so afraid of his uncontrolled strength.

He was breathing unsteadily, his eyes closed, his forehead resting against hers.

She smoothed the dark hair at his nape gently and relaxed completely, absorbing his formidable weight. He was calming. The rigidity of his muscular body was slowly giving way.

"So that's what it's like," she murmured, awed.

Her tone dragged a strained laugh from his throat. "Didn't you know?"

"Not really," she confessed. Her eyes closed. "Puzzles," she said.

He caught his breath at the word picture she evoked. "Yes," he managed. "Except that this particular one can be difficult to fit together, unless it's put into place with exquisite tenderness."

Her arms linked around his neck. His chest was damp and cool against hers as the heat began to die out of them.

"Am I too heavy?" he asked.

"Oh, no. I like the way it feels."

He nuzzled his face against hers. "How about a swim, while we're here?"

"I don't have a bathing suit," she said absently.

He lifted his head. "Neither do I. We're being married in two days, Anna. I want you to know it all before I put my ring on your finger."

The thought of seeing him without his clothes disturbed her, but she sensed that for him this was an obstacle that frightened him. As he said, they were going to be married. Many engaged couples did much more together than just swim without their clothes.

"All right," she said softly.

Evan caught his breath. "Are you sure?"

"Yes." She touched his mouth with her fingertips. "I love you."

So she said. But he wanted proof. If she could look at him without fear, one hurdle would be out of the way. Louisa's face still haunted him.

"So be it," he said quietly.

He got to his feet and helped her up, noticing her shy reluctance to undress in front of him. He smiled gently. "I'll walk down the path a bit. Yell when you're in the water."

She sighed. "Thank you, Evan."

"You'll get used to it," he replied. He brushed a kiss across her mouth and moved away.

She was in the water when he came back, and she kept her eyes averted while he took off his own clothes. Seconds later there was a splash as he landed close beside her.

"Not so difficult, was it?" he asked with a grin as she trod water beside him.

"I guess the first time is the hardest," she mused.

"And the most necessary. Come on, chicken. I'll race you."

She laughed, catching up with him. They played lazily. The feel of the water against her skin was exquisite. She closed her eyes and floated, glorying in the sense of freedom she felt.

Evan watched her with hungry eyes, his heart pounding as he got fascinating glimpses of her creamy body under the water. When she arched her back and began to float, her taut nipples breaking the surface of the lake, he was totally lost.

"Oh, God," he groaned softly.

He reached for her, pulling her body totally against his as he bent to her lips.

She let him kiss her, feeling for the first time the touch of his body with no fabric to conceal its power and strength. She hesitated, and he lifted his head.

"Afraid of me like this?" he whispered.

"Not afraid, really," she confessed. Her blue eyes searched his dark ones. "I've never been without my clothes in front of anyone since I grew up—not even my mother."

He held her waist in his big hands and searched her eyes. "I won't hurt you. Try to remember that."

As he spoke, he lifted and turned her, carrying her toward the bank. She gasped and buried her embarrassed face in his cool throat.

His mouth slid across her cheek to her lips and he began to kiss her with exquisite tenderness. After a minute, she forgot her nudity and gave in to the delicious pleasure of skin against skin.

She felt the jolt of his body as he walked, then the cool air on her body and the softness of the grass on her back as he laid her down.

He knelt over her, waiting for her eyes to open.

She looked at him, flushed and looked away.

He stiffened. "Don't you want to scream and run?" he asked tersely. "She did."

The bitterness in his voice knocked the shyness right out of her. She forced her embarrassed eyes back to his powerful body, reminding herself that in two more days he was going to be her husband. She had to grow up, very fast.

Her lips parted as she looked at him, and her heart began to race. She'd never seen a centerfold, but she was certain that he would have made a perfect one.

Her rapt stare drained some of the apprehension from him. Her eyes were shy and frankly fascinated, but not afraid.

He was doing some looking of his own. A woman's body was no mystery to him, but Anna's was enough to make a hardened womanizer crazy. Her soft curves were perfect, all of her, from the thrust of her breasts to the sweeping curve of her hips and her long, elegant legs.

The sight of her aroused him, and he didn't turn away

or try to hide the effect she had on him. She had to face that as well.

Her breath came unsteadily through her lips. "Oh, my," she whispered.

He lifted an eyebrow, waiting to see if she was bluffing.

After a minute, her gaze lifted from his body to his eyes. "You thought I'd be afraid if I saw you like this," she said suddenly.

"Yes."

She smiled shyly. "I'm sorry to disappoint you," she said, watching the way his eyes followed hungrily the sensuous lines of her body. "Why don't you come down here and kiss me?"

He could barely breathe, much less speak. "Because if I do, I won't be able to stop."

"We're going to be married day after tomorrow."

"Yes," he agreed. "And we're going to have a wedding night. A conventional one, with all the trimmings."

He managed to drag himself to his feet. He fished a couple of towels out of the trunk of his car and tossed one to a subdued Anna.

"Spoilsport," she managed with a shy laugh.

With a muttered curse of pure frustrated anguish, he pulled on his clothes and lit a cigarette while she was still fumbling with hooks and snaps.

She watched him quietly when she had finished. He was remembering the past, she knew. She'd always thought of him as a gentle giant. The idea of Evan hurting anything or anyone deliberately had never occurred to her.

"You can't be afraid of people you love," she said gently.

He grimaced, glancing at her. "Can't you? She was."

She went close to him. "There's something you don't know yet, Evan."

"What?" he asked huskily, remembering the incredible beauty of her body as he looked down at her.

"If Louisa had loved you—really loved you—she couldn't have been afraid of you in bed."

He flushed. "She loved me," he said doggedly.

"Did she?" She turned and picked up the towels, folding them neatly. He was preoccupied all the way back to the car.

He put her in the front seat and got in beside her. There was a terrible truth in what she'd said. He hated the implications of it, that he'd wasted years of his life, years of happiness he might have had with Anna, brooding over a love affair that must have been nothing more than a brief infatuation for Louisa. His great love affair had ended in tragedy, only because he couldn't recognize what Anna seemed to know instinctively—that Louisa had never loved him in the first place. It was a hard pill to swallow.

# Chapter 11

They were married on Friday afternoon, with Evan's entire family in attendance. It was a brief but beautiful ceremony, and Anna could hardly believe she was actually marrying Evan, even after he had slid the diamond-studded gold band that matched her solitaire onto her finger and kissed her tenderly.

But despite that tenderness, he was worried. During the small reception at the Tremayne home, he was preoccupied. Anna alone knew why. He was dreading his wedding night, so haunted by the past that he was certain he was going to send her screaming from him. She knew better, but she had to convince Evan that his great strength wasn't dangerous in intimacy.

"It was a beautiful wedding, darling," Polly told her daughter just before Anna and Evan left on their brief honeymoon to New Orleans. "I hope you'll be happy."

"I will be," Anna replied. She kissed and hugged her

mother, then glanced toward her father, who was talking to Evan and Harden. "How about you and Dad?"

Polly grinned. "He has to fly back to Atlanta tonight."

"Oh." Anna's face fell.

"I'm flying back with him," Polly continued, laughing at Anna's shocked face. "He's going to ask for a transfer to Houston so that he can be home nights when he's not scheduled on flights. We're going to be a family again, Anna. And when Duke retires—which he's planning to do next year—I may get out of the real estate business and travel around the country with him."

"It's almost too good to be true." Anna sighed, smiling through tears. "I'm so happy!"

"So am I," Polly replied. She dried Anna's tears. "Go and have a nice honeymoon. When you're back, with both feet on the ground, we'll talk. Take care of yourself."

"You, too."

Minutes later, Anna was sitting beside Evan as he drove them to the airport.

"Happy?" he asked gently, glancing at her.

"Very. Are you?"

"Ask me in the morning," he said with a rough laugh.

"Oh, Evan." She sighed. "Am I going to have to get you drunk and seduce you?"

He didn't laugh. His face hardened. "That wasn't funny."

"I'm not afraid of you," she said gently.

"I hope not. Because tonight, you'll get to prove it."

She gave up trying to reassure him and stared out the window. Her wedding day had fallen flat, and the honeymoon had barely started.

New Orleans was brassy and colorful, and once Anna had rested for a few minutes, she and a subdued Evan went out to explore the French Quarter and Bourbon Street. It was late afternoon when they got back to the hotel, and Evan herded her right into the restaurant for supper before they went up to their room. During the meal she tried to make conversation, but he was heavy weather. And if she thought things couldn't be worse, she was mistaken.

When they got up to their room, she turned to kiss him, but he actually backed away.

"No," he said shortly, his dark eyes antagonistic. "Not now."

"We're married, Evan," she said gently. "It's all right."

"The hell it is." He grabbed up his Stetson and went toward the door. "I've got a business meeting. I'll be late, so don't wait up."

"A business meeting? On our honeymoon!" she wailed.

He wouldn't look at her. He'd let his anxiety build until he was terrified to touch her. He couldn't admit that. The next best thing was to invent an excuse to get away from her until he could get a grip on himself.

"Sorry," he replied. "It couldn't be helped. I'll be back when I can. Good night."

He closed the door. Anna sat down on the bed with a thud and gaped after him. She wondered how she was going to survive marriage with a man who was afraid to touch her. Damn Louisa!

She finally slept, but not until the wee hours of the morning. When she drifted off, Evan still hadn't come to bed, and she'd cried until her eyes were red.

Meanwhile, Evan was sitting in a bar, drinking whiskey, trying to convince himself that he wasn't King Kong. Anna loved him. She wasn't Louisa. But she was innocent, and he knew all too well how delicate an innocent woman's body was. He was helpless when he started kissing her. If he lost control, he knew he was going to hurt her. He loved her until he thought his heart would break. He took another swallow, and another, brooding over all the times his strength had intimidated men and women alike. Before he knew it, the bar was empty. He paid for his drinks and went slowly up to their room, wondering whether Anna was asleep yet.

The next morning, she woke, vaguely aware that she wasn't alone in the bed. She rolled over and found Evan.

With a faint sigh, she propped up on her elbow and looked at him. Asleep, he seemed younger and much less dangerous. Poor, tormented man. She couldn't really blame him for those mental scars. A man's ego was his most vulnerable spot, after all.

But they really couldn't go on like this.

It seemed underhanded somehow to take advantage of a man in his sleep, but Anna knew instinctively that Evan's irrational fear of hurting her was going to make any other course of action impossible.

She tugged off her nightgown and smiled as she looked down on his sleeping face. With any luck at all she could make him believe he was only dreaming. Of course, she'd have to do it just the right way....

Dawn was only beginning in the eastern sky, so that there was barely any light in the room. Carefully she pulled the sheet down and threw it off the bed, her breath catching at the sight of Evan's body. He was already aroused, and he began to move restlessly, as if just the brush of the sheet had excited him.

She eased down, her mouth slowly touching his broad chest, teasing his nipples. They were already hard, and she felt his breathing change as she nibbled at them. Her hands slid over the broad expanse of his hair-roughened chest and down his flanks to his hard thighs. As her hands moved, so did her mouth. She kissed him tenderly, nipped at him with her teeth, until she reached his navel and the sudden rippling of muscles just beneath it.

His back arched sensuously and he moaned. She turned her face, so that her long hair brushed across his hips and thighs, and he whispered her name.

She nipped at his waist with her teeth while her fingers slowly, torturously made their way up his powerful legs to his flat stomach.

Seconds later, she felt herself lifted and turned, felt his mouth catch and half swallow her breast, his tongue rough on the hard nipple as he began to suckle her.

She shivered with delight, holding his head to her body. His hands were smoothing over her, learning her. One slid between her thighs and coaxed her legs apart.

He touched her then in a way he never had before, and she gasped at the unexpected surge of pleasure the exquisitely slow movements of his fingers aroused. All the while, his mouth was warm on her taut breast, drawing the nipple into the moist darkness with devastating expertise.

Her eyes closed as she let the pleasure wash over her. Her body twisted sinuously under his hands and mouth, soft moans whispering out of her throat while the minutes grew hotter and more feverish.

His mouth gently covered hers while his fingers trespassed in a new and frightening way. There was a brief flash of pain and she moaned, but his mouth gentled her, moving lovingly from her lips to her closed eyelids while his hand began to rouse her all over again. The pain was quickly forgotten as her hips began to lift toward those tormenting fingers.

She felt his breath on her lips, just before he whispered

her name. Her eyes opened slowly, half-dazed, and met his.

Holding them, he moved slowly between her legs, levering down carefully. "No, don't look away," he said shakily.

She swallowed, because she could feel him now in an intimacy unlike anything they'd ever shared. He was much more potent than she remembered, powerful and a little intimidating.

"Hold on," he murmured. "Dig your nails into me, if it helps."

She gasped as his hips arched down into hers, very carefully. He pushed, softly, and she tensed despite her resolve.

"Shh," he whispered, his eyes tender. "You knew it would be difficult. But you can take me. Try to relax. Try to let your body absorb mine. Think of a stone falling into water," he said softly as he moved. "Absorb me, little one. Take me…inside you."

The imagery was arousing. She drew her eyes down to their bodies and caught her breath at what she saw.

"No, don't look there," he said gently, convinced even now that she was going to panic. "Look at me, Anna."

She lifted her eyes back up to his, but there was no fear in them. She arched her back, her breath catching, her eyes misty now with desire. "I watched," she said unsteadily. "Evan, I saw…!"

She pushed harder, absorbing him. There was a burning sensation, a stabbing pain. She cried out, but she pushed harder. And then it was easy. Slow. Soft.

Her breathing began to quicken and she managed a smile as she sought his eyes. "Oh…yes!" she moaned, shaking as she experienced the full power of his masculinity.

He let out a ragged breath. "Yes." He bent to her lips as

his body began the slow, familiar rhythm. He nibbled her mouth as his muscles tautened, as his hips lifted and fell with exquisite tenderness.

Her fingers slid to the base of his spine and lingered, stroking him. He shuddered. She liked that, so she did it again.

"Stop," he ground out. "You'll make me lose control."

"I want you to," she whispered with a tiny smile, arching her mouth up to his. "Let go," she breathed at his lips. "Let go, Evan. It's all right, darling, you won't hurt me. It's all right. Let go, Evan…let go…!"

"Anna!" Her name was a tormented groan as he gave in to her coaxing and suddenly drove feverishly for fulfillment. He lost his fear of hurting her and every vestige of control, in the violent need to experience ecstasy, to satisfy the throbbing, savage ache in his loins.

Even through her own building pleasure, Anna watched him achieve it. As she felt the crush of his arms and the weight of him, she saw his torso lift, his back arch tautly, his face contort as if with the most incredible kind of agony. He threw back his head and cried out, shuddering against her so violently that she thought he might actually lose consciousness.

When he stiffened and fell heavily against her, she was still shivering with her own unsatisfied need. She clutched at his broad shoulders, biting him helplessly as she moved under his weight. When he started to lift his hips, she caught them with her nails and held him there.

"No, please…!" she sobbed.

"Almost, but not quite, is that it, sweetheart?" he whispered huskily. "Give me your mouth, little one, and hold on tight. I'll satisfy you completely, now."

She turned her face up and he kissed her gently, his

tongue suddenly stabbing into her mouth as his hips rose and fell slowly.

It took only seconds. She sobbed her pleasure under his mouth, so racked by ecstasy that she could only cling to him while the rhythm wrung every last silvery bit of strength out of her.

He kissed the tears away, but she still wouldn't let go of him.

"All right," he whispered, smiling through his exhaustion as he settled back over her, his forearms catching his weight. He kissed her gently, soft kisses that calmed and soothed and comforted. All that worry, he thought ruefully, and for nothing! He hadn't killed her after all, even if, for a few delicious seconds, she had sounded as though she were dying.

"Don't go away," she whispered. "Hold me."

He kissed her very gently. "It was for your own sake that I was moving away, not for mine. I thought you might be uncomfortable. It was difficult for you."

Her arms contracted. "I love you," she whispered. "It was heaven."

"For me, too." He sighed softly and rested his cheek against hers, his eyes closed as he savored her softness under him. "Are you all right? It didn't hurt too much?"

"No." She nibbled at his earlobe. "Now will you stop running from me?"

"Do I have a choice?" He looked down at her tenderly. "You took me without fear," he said, his voice coloring with pride and pleasure.

"Yes." She blushed a little and dropped her eyes to his mouth.

"None of that." He tilted her face up and searched her shy eyes. "I didn't hold back. I couldn't. We never discussed precautions…"

Her face brightened. "I could be pregnant."

The way she said it made his heart lift. "Yes." He smoothed back her long, soft blond hair. "You're very young."

"Not that young." She lifted herself to his mouth and began to kiss him, slowly, seductively.

"It's too soon," he said huskily. "You need time to get over what we just did."

She did, but she hated the thought of giving up the closeness they were sharing. Her eyes told him so.

"Come here." He wrapped her up against him and pulled the sheet over them, pausing to brush a kiss across her nose before his arm contracted around her, bringing her even closer. "We'll sleep a bit longer."

"And then?" she whispered.

He smiled. "And then."

She closed her own eyes, sliding into a deep and dreamless sleep. When she awoke, the smell of beignets— little square sugar-dusted doughnuts—and jam and fresh coffee filled the room.

"Hungry?" Evan asked. He was wearing his slacks and nothing else, and he looked younger and lighthearted and totally loving. That could have been a trick of the light, of course, she told herself. But she could dream.

"I'm starved," she confessed, sitting up.

He pulled the sheet away and looked at her, his eyes darkening with possession. "My God, you are so beautiful," he said, his voice deep and uneven.

"Flatterer," she whispered softly.

He sat down beside her, his eyes searching hers while his hands stroked slowly down her body. She caught her breath and stiffened with pleasure and he bent to kiss the hardened tips of her breasts.

But when she tried to trap his mouth against her, he shook his head and pulled away. "It's too soon for you," he said, his eyes full of tender wisdom. "We've got the rest of our lives to love each other in bed."

"It felt like that," she said softly. "Like…loving, I mean."

"Shouldn't it?" he asked, his eyes holding hers. "When two people love each other as much as we do?"

Her heart stopped beating. "You…don't," she whispered.

"Then why did I marry you, little one?" he asked quietly. "If sex was all I wanted, any woman would have done."

She thought she might faint.

"I was trying to spare you what Louisa suffered at my hands." He smiled bitterly. "She never loved me, Anna. And I never knew it. Until you told me."

Her breath was trapped somewhere in her throat.

He touched her face with a big, gentle hand. "I was sacrificing my happiness for what I thought was yours. After what Louisa had said to me, I was terrified of hurting you like that. And you were so young… But when Randall told me you were marrying him, I thought I'd go mad." He choked. "That was bad enough. But you were mugged, and I didn't even know it until hours later. You could have died, and I wouldn't have been there, with you. Your last memory of me would have been of the way I'd hurt you," he said roughly.

Tears stung her eyes. What he felt was naked in his face, in his voice. Why hadn't she seen it, known it? "You…love me!" she exclaimed, awed.

"Love. Adore. Worship." He framed her face in his hands and kissed her with aching tenderness. "Oh, God, you're the very breath in my body!"

He bore her down on the mattress, his mouth ardent and faintly rough with passion, his hands insistent on her body as he kissed her. She gave unstintingly, loving him so deeply that it hurt.

"I love you," he whispered finally, his mouth against her throat. "I'll die loving you."

She held him, her eyes closed, her heart overflowing. "I love you, too, Evan," she said drowsily. "Endlessly."

He bent again to her mouth, the look in his eyes before he kissed her so adoring that she melted under him. The kiss went on and on and on, into levels they'd never touched before.

Finally he managed to drag himself away. "You'd better eat something," he murmured, his voice faintly unsteady. "I have to build up your strength for the next few days, after you've had time to recuperate."

She laughed and looked up at him. "That goes double for you," she murmured demurely. "You're not the only one with expectations."

He burst out laughing. A minute later he picked her up in his big arms and carried her to the breakfast table. For the first time he gloried in his strength, in her trusting submission to it. All the ghosts were laid to rest, now. He looked down at her, so soft in his arms, and felt as if he had everything. He sat down at the table with Anna cuddled in his lap. Not content with that, he spoon-fed her every single bite.

From that moment on, they were inseparable, and every day brought a new and ardent memory. Anna's nightmares faded, and her painful experience with the mugger became nothing more than a bad dream. Weeks later, a big, brutal man was found in a back alley dead of a drug overdose. He was a suspect in several violent robberies in Houston, the paper said, and at least one rape. A violent end for a violent man, but his death gave Anna peace.

Polly and Duke settled down to a happy life together, while Anna and Evan moved into a newly remodeled house on the Tremayne ranch, a wedding present from Evan's brothers. It included a studio for Anna, and she went back to her painting with a vengeance. But in addition to her landscapes she did one portrait—of her new husband.

"Do I really look like that?" he asked dryly as he clasped her loosely by the waist and looked over her shoulder at the very flattering painting.

"To me, you do," she said, her eyes full of love.

He smiled before he bent to kiss her. The old specter of his size and strength were gone forever. Secure in the warmth of Anna's love, he couldn't have asked for another single thing, a sentiment she echoed with her whole heart.

\* \* \* \* \*

# THE Essential COLLECTION

## by Diana Palmer

**YES!** Please send me *The Essential Collection* by Diana Palmer. This collection will begin with 3 FREE BOOKS and 2 FREE GIFTS in my very first shipment—and more valuable free gifts will follow! My books will arrive in 8 monthly shipments until I have the entire 51-book *Essential Collection* by Diana Palmer. I will receive 2 free books in each shipment and I will pay just $4.49 U.S./$5.39 CDN for each of the other 4 books in each shipment, plus $2.99 for shipping and handling.* If I decide to keep the entire collection, I'll only have paid for 32 books because 19 books are free. I understand that accepting the 3 free books and gifts places me under no obligation to buy anything. I can always return a shipment and cancel at any time. My free books and gifts are mine to keep no matter what I decide.

279 HDK 9860    479 HDK 9860

| Name | (PLEASE PRINT) | |
| --- | --- | --- |

| Address | | Apt. # |
| --- | --- | --- |

| City | State/Prov. | Zip/Postal Code |
| --- | --- | --- |

Signature (if under 18, a parent or guardian must sign)

### Mail to the **Reader Service:**
**IN U.S.A.:** P.O. Box 1867, Buffalo, NY 14240-1867
**IN CANADA:** P.O. Box 609, Fort Erie, Ontario L2A 5X3

* Terms and prices subject to change without notice. Prices do not include applicable taxes. Sales tax applicable in N.Y. Canadian residents will be charged applicable taxes. This offer is limited to one order per household. All orders subject to credit approval. Credit or debit balances in a customer's account(s) may be offset by any other outstanding balance owed by or to the customer. Please allow 4–6 weeks for delivery. Offer available while quantities last. Offer not available to Quebec residents.

**Your Privacy**—The Reader Service is committed to protecting your privacy. Our Privacy Policy is available online at www.ReaderService.com or upon request from the Reader Service.

We make a portion of our mailing list available to reputable third parties that offer products we believe may interest you. If you prefer that we not exchange your name with third parties, or if you wish to clarify or modify your communication preferences, please visit us at www.ReaderService.com/consumerschoice or write to us at Reader Service Preference Service, P.O. Box 9062, Buffalo, NY 14269. Include your complete name and address.